John George Ryan

Life and Adventures of Gen. W. A. C. Ryan

The Cuban Martyr

John George Ryan

Life and Adventures of Gen. W. A. C. Ryan
The Cuban Martyr

ISBN/EAN: 9783337379315

Printed in Europe, USA, Canada, Australia, Japan

Cover: Foto ©Raphael Reischuk / pixelio.de

More available books at **www.hansebooks.com**

LIFE AND ADVENTURES

OF

GEN. RYAN,

THE CUBAN MARTYR.

BY AN OLD COMRADE.

SCULLY & COMPANY, PUBLISHERS,

CHICAGO AND NEW YORK.

1876.

LIFE AND ADVENTURES

OF

GEN. W. A. C. RYAN.

THE CUBAN MARTYR.

CAPTURED ON THE STEAMER VIRGINIUS, AND
MURDERED BY THE SPANIARDS AT
SANTIAGO, CUBA, NOV. 4, 1873.

Comprising four years in the Cuban Revolution
—Four years in the U. S. Army, during the
War in the United States—His adventures in the
wilds of Montana—Startling escapades—Interesting family history—Etc. Together with
sketches of the lives of Generals Varona, Del
Sol, Cespedes, Capt. Fry, and others.

BY AN OLD COMRADE.

The dying words of Secretary of War Rawlins—"Poor Cuba
should be free."

NEW YORK AND CHICAGO.
1876.

Publisher's Notice.

The manuscript of the "Life and adventures of General Ryan" was presented to the undersigned for publication, that it might be the means of assisting the friends of the dead hero to carry out their design of having a monument erected to his memory. In presenting the work to the public he does so with considerable trepidation—because of a few slight errors that were overlooked by the proof-reader, and which were not discovered until after the pages were stereotyped—and craves indulgence of the intelligent reader for the unintentional shortcomings. Being a newspaper man himself, he feels certain that his brethren of the press will lend their generous aid to have the object of the book made a grand success, and to their consideration he specially appeals in the premises.

JOHN GEO. RYAN.

September, 1876.

2

CONTENTS.

Contents. **v**

This work is dedicated
to the memory of the heroes of
the late war in the United States,
and the present one in Cuba,
who died for principle.

LIFE

OF

General Ryan.

———•———

" They never fail who die
In a great cause; the block may soak their gore,
Their heads may sodden in the sun; their limbs
Be strung from city gates and castle walls;
But still their spirits walk abroad." [BYRON.

•

["Lafayette, Pulaski, DeKalb, Steuben and
Kosciusko were filibusters and pirates, if General
RYAN was."]

Before entering thoroughly upon the narrative of the life of General RYAN, the author
desires to state that he has undertaken a task
which might be more faithfully performed by
a mind erudite and a pen facile and polished;
but in doing so he feels that critics will over-
look his shortcomings, when they become
aware that he aims at no literary merit, but
merely the plain portrayal of interesting facts
in the public career of one who played such a
prominent part in life's great drama, and at
last gave up a promising and brilliant future

7

by falling a willing victim to the glorious cause of Cuba's freedom.   He leaves to a brighter intellect and more florid painter the enviable pleasure of doing full justice to the character of him who was the peer of Lafayette as a patriot, the equal of that grand and glorious soldier, Marshal Ney, as a martyr ; and the would-be equal of the immortal Napoleon I. as a warrior.

The author believes that in this advanced age of intelligence the notable acts of public men should be handed down to posterity in a tangible form, that coming generations may be benefitted thereby.   This is one of the reasons why he contributes these imperfect sketches to the world's literature, that they may furnish a chapter from which the historian may gain some information.   And another is, the performance of a sacred duty to the memory of his dear, murdered friend, comrade in arms, associate in social life, and brave, chivalrous, dashing, handsome, charitable and honest gentleman, under all circumstances ; and who—if he had been spared his cruel fate, and opportunity offered—would have dazzled the world, and held it transfixed in wonderment, as did the mighty luminary he aimed to emulate, history's grandest military genius, he whose sun of glory went down at Waterloo, and sank forever upon the sea-washed rocks of St. Helena.

For the principal portion of the materials

used in this work the author acknowledges himself especially indebted to his hero's brother, Col. John Geo. Ryan, of Pine Bluff, Arkansas, a newspaper man, who requests him to return his, the colonel's, sincere and heartfelt thanks to his brethren of the press throughout the country for the many generous remarks passed upon his murdered brother. Gratitude is also due Gen. Martin Beem and Col. W. S. Scribner, of Chicago, Ill., and Capt. John W. Fenton, Washington, D. C., three as gallant soldiers as ever drew sword for libery, and who fought with Gen. Ryan under the stars and stripes during the late rebellion in the United States.

Col. Ryan placed at the author's disposal an immense collection of letters and papers, and a life-time diary of the General. From these, and reminiscences gleaned from the memory of the General's friends, the major portion of the work is compiled.

To dwell at length upon the many interesting incidents here introduced would far exceed the size of this production; even faint elaboration would make a very large volume. However, in time the public may be gratified in this respect.

GENEALOGICAL.

GEN. WILLIAM ALBERT CHARLES RYAN was born March 28, 1843, in Toronto, Canada. Consequently, at the time of his murder, the

4th of Nov., 1873, he had just passed his thirtieth year. He was the third son of a family of four; the fourth, and youngest, being a girl. His father, Capt. John Ryan, was the only son of Major Patrick Ryan who fought in the celebrated Fifth Dragoon Guards under Wellington, and distinguished himself in the historical battles of Waterloo, Salamanca, Corruna, Lorena, the siege of Badajos, and numerous other engagements, coming out of each covered with glory, and often receiving severe wounds.

It is a very remarkable fact that he, our hero's father, was born on the battle-field, in Spain, and under the same flag that floated over and authorized his son's inhuman butchery. The same gun that heralded the commencement of the bloody battle of Salamanca announced the advent of Gen. Ryan's father into this world. In those days it was not an unusual thing for officers' ladies to accompany their husbands to the tented field, and time and again did Mrs. Major Ryan hear the awful clash of battle, and witness the terrible carnage after each bloody conflict while nursing the to-be father of the illustrious Cuban martyr. The adventures of this lady were many, romantic and interesting while in the tented field, under danger of the screeching shell, or on the long and dreary march; and her relation of them immensely delighted her heroic grandson when a mere boy. She was

held in such high esteem as to be, when in
foreign lands, entrusted with the army's
money. On one occasion, while in Portugal,
this fact nearly cost her her life. One of her
escort deserted, and returned with a band of
native robbers who attacked her, for the purpose of plunder. Fortunately a force of dragoons arrived in time to disperse the bandits,
who fled, leaving several of their number behind dead.

The acquaintance of this lady and Major
Ryan was brought about by a remarkably
sad, aye horrible, chapter in her family history. Her father was a Mr. —. Paine, of
the same stock as the illustrious Tom Paine,
the so-called infidel, and brother of the chief
of police of Dublin, and of a church of England minister officiating near that city. During the Irish Rebellion of 1798, it is said that
he was murdered by a Roman Catholic mob.
While the Fifth Dragoon Guards were on
duty guarding Mr. Paine's residence, after
the latter's murder, Major Ryan and Miss
Lizzie Paine formed the acquaintance that
culminated in their marriage. The fact that
Miss Paine became connected with the Roman Catholic church after her marriage,
would seem to belie the statement that her
father was killed for his anti-Catholic professions.

During this season of mourning in the
Paine family another sister and a Captain

Russell, of the Life Guards, formed an attachment that resulted in their union. The descendents of this alliance reside near Montreal, Canada.

These marriages of the Misses Paine, so far as their espousing the Catholic faith, were very much frowned upon by the rest of the family. But the lovers cared not.

GEN. RYAN's mother was named Eliza, a daughter of Mr. Patrick Burke, a well-to-do gentleman of Birr, Kings county, Ireland, in whose veins flowed the same blood that coursed through those of the illustrious Irish orator and statesman of the same name. Her family, also, was of a military turn of mind, and she now has a brother a Captain, or ex-Captain, of the British army, residing in Dublin, in comparative ease. He ran away from school when quite young, joined the British army, went to India, and through a series of brilliant exploits, won his spurs as a Captain. In India he married, and has now around him a happy family. He was held in such high esteem by the British government that one of his sons was complimented with a commission as a military surgeon. He now looks forward to the early promotion of a gallant young nephew, Will Manning, a subaltern officer in the artillery in the afar-off torrid East Indies.

GEN. RYAN's father would have followed the army as a profession, if it had not been for the bursting of a blood-vessel at a very early age, which rendered such a course impossible. When a child, he was considered the pet of his father's regiment, because of his intelligent and winning manners. Lord Gough, one of England's brightest soldiers, promised the little fellow a Captaincy, and forever after, in the command, he was known as the "little Captain."

An amusing incident once occurred to the "little Captain." The soldiers desired to have a good time, but had not the pecuniary means to carry out their wishes. Here the "little Captain" was brought into requisition. He consented to be secreted. A general alarm was sounded. The mother was nearly distracted, and offered any amount for his recovery. At last he was found, and the soldiers restoring him each received a pound, equivalent to five dollars of American money. With this fund they made merry, and time and oft toasted their little friend. It was years after, when nearly all the characters in the play had melted into earth, that the episode was made public. This was at a Masonic dinner in London, where high and low members of the craft were assembled. Major Ryan was a Mason of high standing, and was the recipient of a large silver medal from his brethren. On one side of it was engraved the emblems of the order, and on the other the names of the battles in which he had been engaged. This medal descended to General Ryan, and saved his life in one of the battles of the late war in the United States. It was struck by a bullet while on his breast.

After the close of the war, when the iron heel of the great Napoleon was lifted from the neck of Europe, and the iconoclast's star had ceased to dazzle the world, and make his enemies tremble with fear, Major Ryan retired from the strife of battle to the shades of peaceful life, and took up his residence in Birr, Kings county, Ireland, the home of Miss Burke, his future daughter-in-law.

In the course of time Miss Burke, who was considered a very lovely and estimable young lady, and the tall, dashing, handsome and splendid looking "Capt." John Ryan met, and formed an acquaintance that resulted in their marriage.

A tinge of romance attached to this union. To some extent, both families were opposed to it, and endeavored to keep the lovers apart. This opposition only heightened their passion. They met one lovely night, repaired to a Protestant clergyman and got married. This action they immediately hastened to disclose to the "old folks." A scene followed. But the finale was a public marriage by a Catholic clergyman.

This union proved a happy one, and its product was three boys and one girl—Patrick

Burke, John George, Wm. Albert Charles, and Lizzie.

Shortly after the birth of their first child Capt. John Ryan turned his eyes to the afar off West, the great world beyond the broad, blue Atlantic ocean, and in due time left the home of his fathers, and soon found himself and young family breathing the pure air that swept across the beautiful bay that fronts Ontario's pride of a city, Toronto, the birth-place of our hero. He was soon followed by his father and mother, who could not bear being separated from him.

In a few short years Major Ryan was suddenly relieved of his earthly troubles, and passed calmly into the shadowy land, wept over by a loving family, and mourned by a large concourse of friends.

Captain Ryan soon followed his father, and their bodies were laid side by side in the silent tomb, in the little rural cemetery at the Lower Gore, near Toronto, Canada, where ten years later were consigned the remains of Mrs. Major Ryan. General Ryan, a grandson she much loved, assisted at the last sad ceremony.

THE QUARTETTE.

The family of Captain Ryan prospered in health, and grew up to man's estate. At this writing, 1876, the eldest, Patrick Burke, is residing in Joliet, Illinois, surrounded by a bright little family, and beloved by a host of friends; and especially by his Masonic brethren. Miss Lizzie is now the wife of Mr. T. A. Kelly, a merchant of Chicago, Illinois, to whom she has borne five lovely children, two boys and three girls. Col. John George resides in Arkansas. He will appear in another chapter. Being closely allied with his lamented brother, the General, he will be here and there scattered throuhhout this narrative to its close.

GEN. RYAN'S FATHER'S DEATH.

After Capt. Ryan's death Mrs. Ryan was suddenly called to Ireland to attend to some matters relating to her father's estate in which she was personally and pecuniarily interested. She remained away two years.

During the mother's absence P. Burke and Lizzie were entrusted to the care of their paternal grandmother, residing on her farm near Toronto; and John George and William Albert Charles were placed in charge of their mother's brother, P. Burke, then, and now, editor and proprietor of the *Dispatch*, St. Thomas, Ontario, Canada, a very worthy gentleman. This was about 1852. It was while with their uncle that both the boys received that nucleus of a knowledge of the printing business, and groundwork of a good moral and general schoolastic education, that enabled them to battle against the trials of

their maturer years. Before they were res-
pectively eleven and thirteen they each could
set and distribute 7000 ems of type per day.
Most of the old residents of St. Thomas will
remember the bright little fellows who carried them their paper, twenty years ago, in
sunshine or rain. One of them was our hero,
Gen. Ryan.

In the summer of 1854 the mother returned
from Europe and took up her residence in
Toronto, and gathered once more to her
heart her four interesting children. Although
the dark cloud, consequent upon the loss of
her husband, that hung over head seemed
ominous for her future, still it had a silver
lining in the sunny faces of her bright little
ones.

FIRST EXPERIENCE WITH "ARTILLERY."

To show at what an early age our hero developed a talent for dabbling with dangerous
things, the following incident will fully illustrate. In the main it is interesting. General
Ryan was only eight years old at the time:

Shortly after their father's death, and dur-
a temporary absence of their mother from
home, Will and Jack, as they were generally
called, concluded to make arrangements to
have a kind of Queen's birthday frolic of
their own. To accomplish this effectually an
old revolutionary musket was "cut down" to
make a cannon. By a picture of one they con-

structed a fort, facing a favorite apple tree, on which a shingle was tacked. At this juncture the "enemy," in the person of their grandmother, suddenly appeared, charged the battery, captured the gun, demolished the works, and made the boys prisoners. For safe keeping, the cannon was thrown into the well.

This discomforture only sharpened their appetites, and at the same time their wits.

A council of war was held in the barn, and it was developed that the other piece of the musket could be utilized by having lead melted into it to form a breech, etc., and that by the "house folks" finding no eggs on the premises for several days a good supply of ammunition could be procured. Money was scarce with boys in those days. For two days it was a profound mystery to the "old lady" why no eggs could be found, notwithstanding the fact that the domestic fowl did its usual amount of cackling. The fault was due to "them neighbors."

In due time everything was ready for the grand blow out. One morning the old lady was supposed to be absent. But she was indoors, closeted away from "them noisy boys." This was glorious for the embryo artillerymen. The fortification was hurriedly erected, the cannon loaded with powder and shot to the muzzle, and planted, the target placed on the tree, and everything made ready. The boys were in the highest glee.

As Jack was about to "turn her loose" Will told him to stop, that he was not in the right position; that he should, like the man in the picture, stand beside, instead of behind the cannon. This close attention to details no doubt saved Jack's life. Jack changed position, and bang she went. The report was loud and startling. When the smoke died away the tree was found shattered, the fortification demolished, and the gun dismounted. The boys looked at each other in speechless wonder. But they soon came to their senses, and just in time to flee, and escape the wrath of their incensed grandame, who was rapidly moving on their position, with evident intention of striking their rear and cutting off their retreat. But her Waterloo tactics were futile for their capture, and she had to be content with the other fruits of victory.

The serious feature of this escapade, and which made the old madam think another battle of Salamanca was being inaugurated, was the startling fact that the big slug of lead that formed the cannon's breech was blown out at the discharge, and sent crashing right through the door, near which she was quietly seated reading, and a few inches from her head, tearing away a long sliver of wood, and wound up by smashing the mirror in which the old lady used to admire her venerable but truly comely person.

It will also be seen that if it was not for

our young hero's quick discernment in alter-
ing his brother's position, that worthy's brilliant career would have been suddenly closed,
by the mass of metal striking his center, and
hurrying him off to join the angels.

It is needless to state that after this exploit
an abundance of eggs could be found, as
usual, about the premises.

Gen. Ryan used to relate this incident with
considerable gusto, while sitting by the camp-
fires during the dreary night-watches of the
war of the great rebellion.

FIRST ATTEMPT TO GO SOLDIERING.

To further show to what an inordinate degree our hero was naturally possessed by the
desire for military life and the pomp of war,
it is only necessary to give another incident
in his boyhood's life.   In the summer of
1855 the British government had recruiting
officers in Canada enlisting men for her forces
in the East Indies.   The recruiting sergeants
held out all sorts of seductive inducements to
entice into their trap the unwary.   A grand
display of flags, ribbons, gay uniforms, and
lively music, together with marvelous tales
of the wonders of that remote torrid country,
were features of the pleasing picture.   As a
matter of course, this aroused the latent fire
in our hero's breast, and fanned it into a
blaze.   At this time he was not thirteen years

of age, but was quite tall. As the recruiting party marched along King street, on their way to the barracks, our hero stood irresolute for a time on the corner, gazing on them. At last he gave way, and stepped into the ranks, and marched to headquarters. His chair was vacant at his mother's table that noon. In the afternoon he came marching in to that astonished lady, who became horrified when she learned the true cause of "her boy" being bedecked with rbibons. After getting over her excitement, she marched the "young gentleman" to a cab, and was driven to the barracks, where she had him transmogrified into a civilian once more, much to his chagrin, as he confidentially told his brother J. G. that evening, because he desired to "become a soldier, and fight his way to fame, like Napoleon."

Down, again, he had to get to his books, after his gay coccade had been laid aside—a task he despised, so far as the school-room routine was concerned.

He loved to read romance, poetry, song, travels, biographies of distinguished military men, and of characters like that noble soul, Robert Emmett. He read incessantly, and his memory was so retentive that he could, after two readings, repeat correctly any ordinary-sized song. He was so fond of reading that often he has been found lying on the floor of a morning, and his book beside him, having read so late that nature gave out and he toppled over. He was enraptured with Milton, Shakspeare, Byron, Moore and Longfellow. Tragic, heroic and sublime verse were his favorites ; still he revelled at times in the entrancing bowers of Moore's song, and was constantly humming, "Remember the glories of Brian, the brave," which, after his murder, his newspaper friends, in speaking of him, changed into "Ryan, the brave." He was, also, passicnately interested in the sad fate of that great warrior, Marshal Ney. The dashing and chivalric Murat, and Lord Byron's "Corsair," were among his idols; and Napoleon was his earthly deity.

These few facts are introduced to show that the statements of many prominent men are not far wrong that General Ryan was a born soldier; and inherited from his ancestors those traits of military genius that placed one so young so very conspicuous before the whole world.

CLOUDS GATHERING.

When least expected by the children, and most certainly not thought of by their loving parent, in the latter part of 1855, a circumstance occurred that changed the current of Mrs. Ryan's happiness, until death—21 years later, at the time of this writing, 1876—relieved her of a terrible burden.

This calamity was her second marriage. Her new partner soon fell under the base influence of the demon alcohol, and turned the family paradise into a house of sorrow and tears. He prostituted good health and a fine education at the shrine of Bacchus, and gathered around his home black clouds, and scattered away the sunshine that was wont to preside there. His name is omitted here out of regard for the memory of General RYAN, who abhorred him. He is dead now, and the great I Am will judge whether or not his heart prompted his miserable conduct toward his wife and her little family, and the vail of charity will here be thrown over his sad record.

One October night, in 1867 it is believed, the storm that had been so long brewing broke forth in all its fury, and when the angry winds lulled to a sigh, Mrs. Ryan found herself alone with him who should have made her happy, instead of miserable. Her children had to flee from the parental roof and go out into the bleak world to seek a home and friends, and she was miserable. It appears that the stepfather, while in his cups, violently assaulted J. G. This the latter quickly resented by felling his powerful assailant to the floor with a heavy iron poker. This act capped the climax, and J. G. left that house hurriedly through a window at the end of two sheets, tied together by his affrighted mother.

The family nest was now effectually broken up; the young had taken flight, and the vulture and the dove only remained. The children and their mother never met together, at one time, afterward, but she continued to pray and watch, and suffer, and wait until God in His mercy lifted her load and bade her arise and walk forth free, no longer the drunkard's wife.

But when this rejoicing came her idolized boy had been snatched away, ruthlessly torn from her loving heart by the red-handed Spaniard, and she was left wrapped up in deepest woe.

INTO THE DARKNESS.

The night of this domestic brawl was frightful without. The winds howled and moaned, and the rain rushed through the black shroud of night like a roaring avalanche, cold and drenching. Into this dreary turmoil stepped J. G. and our hero. "It was an awful night," said Gen. Ryan; "the winds howled most dismally, the thunder loudly roared and crashed, the lightning flitted frightfully through the inky darkness, like countless meteors, and the rain fell in a perfect sluice. I thought the end of time had come as we three, mother, brother and I, stood shivering there under the poor shelter of a small tree, while in the dim distance could be seen the lamp's flicker, as that madman of a stepfather rushed through the house looking for us."

While the elements warred thus savagely the wretched mother and her two children groped their way through the darkness to a friend's welcome shelter, where they spent the night.

During the enactment of this distasteful little drama the other two children were on a visit to their grandmother in the country.

AFTERWARD HANGED.

As the trio were hurrying along through the pitiless storm a little figure, carrying a lantern, joined them, and helped guide their steps through the darkness and mud. It was young Fleming, a friend of the boys, and a telegraph messenger. He was a bright, intelligent boy, and had worked himself out of the filthiest purlieus of society to his present position. He was a courteous and honest lad, and a favorite with the operators. Displaying a talent for the cabalistic profession, these gentlemen assisted his efforts, and soon he ceased to deliver messages and was promoted as assistant operator. Thus he advanced, until he arrived at the top of the ladder, being considered the best " sound " operator in the country. In those days " sound " operators were among the wonders. Now he was very much envied by the dirty tribe he herded

with when a child, because he would not join
in their vile orgies. Fortune continued to
lavish her favors on him. Her was appointed
to the managership of the Montreal office,
and was to leave the next day. He never
went. That night he was insulted and assaulted by a ruffian of his early-day acquaintance. In defending himself he drove a knife
to his heart, and he fell dead. Poor Fleming
was arraigned and tried for murder in the
first degree, and convicted. Notwithstanding
the efforts of his friends to mollify the law, the
unfortunate young fellow was hanged to death
outside of the high wall of the old stone jail
in Toronto, one gloomy, drizzling morning in
the fall of 1857. Upon none fell more heavily
this sad news than on our hero. Strange,
both so promising, and each came to an unnatural death.

LEAVING HOME.

The day after the domestic wrangle the
mother concluded to accede to the boys' wish
to go to the States, notwitstanding the pang
it would cause her heart. W. A. C. mapped
out the lovely city of Buffalo for his future
home, while J. G. cast his eyes away southward, and let them rest upon New Orleans,
the great metropolis of the sunny south, the
cradle of chivalry and refinement, beautiful
women, sweet flowers and soft blue skies.
In that lovely region he had some friends,

among whom were the late Joseph Barker,
his banker ; Col. John O. Nixon, the talented
editor of the *Crescent*, and P. Boyle, afterward connected with the Canadian Fenian
excitement, and editor of the *Irish Canadian*,
of Toronto.

W. A. C. had, also, a number of friends in
Buffalo, and around Niagara Falls.

In due time the sad parting took place, the
mother was kissed an adieu, tears were shed,
and the boys started out into the treacherous
world to battle against its many vicissitudes.

The three never met together again.

COL. J. G. RYAN.

We will now leave our hero to his studies
in Buffalo, and hurriedly sketch his brother's
eventful career up to the time they first met,
which was not until June 1867.

After a short stay in the Crescent City he
became connected with the Liberty, Miss.,
Herald, and the old residents of that beautiful little place may yet remember the curley-
haired blonde who used to stroll about with
the tall, dashing brunette, Herbert Poindex-
ter, the chief editor..... Back again to the
seductive charms of voluptuous New Orleans
life.... Then a dangerous siege of Yellow
Jack.... Out of this into the whirling vortex
of the great rebellion, and other ups and

downs, until we find him an Arkansas Colonel of Cavalry.

J. G. soon became thoroughly imbued with southern ideas, and when the war commenced he was one of the first to volunteer. Sickness prevented him accompanying the Third Louisiana in the north Arkansas campaign, so he remained for awhile at Pine Bluff, Ark., where he joined K company of the 18th Arkansas regiment. He was with this command at the siege of Fort Pillow, the battle of Farmington, the skirmishing around Corinth, the retreat from Corinth by Beauregard, the battle of Iuka, and the bloody fight at Corinth Oct. 3rd and 4th, 1862. In this terrible battle he was several times wounded and made prisoner. In May, 1863, he escaped to his friends from Iuka, Miss., hospital prison. When Grierson made his celebrated raid down through Mississippi from Memphis he and Lieutenants Smith, Baird and Daily, and sergeant A. P. Turner, of Crawfordsville, Miss., organized a cavalry squadron, and he was commissioned its Captain. It was a splendid body of young men, but it did not catch the lightning raider. In a few months this and other squadrons were organized into a regiment, the 16th Confederate, Ryan's being the senior. The first battle of this new command was on the 24th of June, 1864, at Lafayette, northwest Georgia. It was in Gen. Pillow's cavalry division, which was soundly whipped. In this he got wounded, at the same time as the gallant Colonel Phil. B. Spence, of Nashville, Tenn., and Gen. O. G. Armistead, of Grenada, Miss. After this "d—d fool mistake of Pillow," to use the expressive language of Colonel Ball, of Alabama, Ryan was placed in command of the forces at Talladega, Ala. But along dashed the Federal General Rousseau and made him fly southward. Now a disturbance with his commanding officer caused him to be sent on special duty in General Dick Taylor's department, where he surrendered, May 12, 1865, at Jackson, Miss. It is to be presumed that the "handsome, curly-haired boy captain," as the little girls styled him, did his duty in the fratricidal conflict, for he had his right leg broken twice by balls, and shot twice below the knee, his right hand perforated twice, his left thumb and cheek struck, and now carries a ball in his right knee and one in his left hip.

THE MYSTERIOUS PRISONER.

After the war Colonel J. G. gained considerable notoriety by his arrest in the Gayoso hotel, Memphis, Tenn., on suspicion of being John H. Surratt, one of those supposed to have been connected with the murder of President Lincoln. He was heavily ironed hand and foot, and stapled down to the floor of that bastile, the Irving block, July 20th. From Memphis he was taken to Washington. Col. Louis B. Smith, of the 3rd United States artillery, lately deceased in Chicago, Ill., and five men of the 120th Illinois volunteers, were his escort. When in Washington he was closely confined in the Old Capitol prison, and part of the time in the "sweat box," a filthy dungeon, merely because he would not disclose the means by which he communicated to Sir Frederick Bruce, the British minister. From Washington he was removed to Prison No. 1, Vicksburg, Miss. There . his chains were removed by General Slocum, who permitted him to communicate with the outer world. From this prison he was released in November, 1865, by order of the war department, without ever having received a trial, hearing, investigation or interrogation.

After his release from prison Colonel Ryan became connected for a time with the Jackson, Miss., *Standard*. Afterward he went to Pine Bluff, Arkansas, and established and ably edited the *Southern Vindicator*, a fiery sheet, and conducted it fearlessly during Governor Clayton's radical reign. After this he edited a Brooks reform paper in Southeast Arkansas, and more subsequently was associate editor of the Pine Bluff *Press*, Col. C. G. Newman's able paper. During his editorial career Col. Ryan had to smell considerable "personal" powder. In these difficulties kansas.'' During the 1874 gubernatorial war in that state, between Baxter and Brooks, the Colonel took the side of Baxter, and was on the staff of the gallant Major Gen. H. King White.

It is learned, from an interview that Col. M. E. Stone, editor of the Chicago *Courier*, had with Col. Ryan, that the latter intends suing the United States government for damages for falsely imprisoning him in 1865. It appears he should be largely indemnified for the monstrous outrage.

—o—

BOOK II.

GEN. RYAN IN THE UNITED STATES ARMY.

It is not necessary to dwell upon the little incidents in our hero's life up to the time of the inauguration of the late great war in the United States, although many of them would be very readable. It is sufficient to say that he had his trials and tribulations ; but during them all he never seemed to lose sight of the idea, as instilled into him by the prognostications of Prof. Fowler, the phrenologist, that there was a future for him tinged with the halo of glory and renown. While in Buffalo he entrusted his enducated to a Mons. Favre Larue, a French-American gentleman, and a finished scholar. As a natural consequence, his association with this gentleman heightened young Ryan's military notions. Under his tutorship he soon became a very good English scholar, and quite expert with the sword and pistol. In after days it was said that he was a regular Paul de Cassagnac with the sword, and a Capt. Travis with the pistol and rifle.

While in Buffalo General RYAN became acquainted with the family of Col. John Fisk, ot Suspension Bridge. He had four nephews, James L., Robert E., Dan. W., and Van, all of whom came out of the war elevated to positions of officers, and covered with coveted honors.

When the tocsin of war sounded, that heralded an attack upon the great sisterhood of states, with a view to divide them, General RYAN joined with these young gentlemen, and his true-to-the-last friend Capt. John W. Fenton, for the purpose of organizing companies of soldiers to march against the nation's foes. His was not the heart to falter when danger threatened the flag he had learned to love. He rallied at the approach of the "first cloud that had gathered over the destiny of this grand nation, established by the greatest men of any age, baptized with the best blood of heaven-born patriots, and handed down to the safe keeping of a noble posterity by heroes who wrested their liberty from the iron jaws of Britain's ferocious lion, by daring to dash forward and rescue it from such polluted keeping."

As the dread alarm spread from sea-coast to mountain top, over peaceful hamlets and rich harvest fields, and while the great heart of the nation throbbed and ached at the awful impending calamity, no cooler counselor was to be found among the young men, who afterward furnished the bone and sinew of the army, than "Whack" Ryan. This anxiety of the people for the nation's weal was at one time, as all know full well, like a sweeping avalanche in its awful earnestness. The dismal blast of warning was echoed and re-echoed until it burst forth like a peal of maddened thunder, and awakened every patriot to the horrible reality that the flag their fathers fought for had been fired upon, the life of the nation threatened, and a bloody and fratricidal war about to be inaugurated by a few discontented malcontents determined to shatter the government into chaotic fragments, in their "idiotic endeavor to set up a kingdom or empire for the perpetuation of the unholy reign of slave power."

AT THE FRONT.

In due time our hero found himself in front

AA

of the enemy, with ample opportunity to display all the ability, natural and acquired that he possessed. He soon learned that glory on paper and in the field are two different and distinct things. He found men worthy of his steel in his enemies, and learned to respect the blades of others, if not their opinions.

When the first sound of the shock of war reached his ear, he was a sergeant in K company, 132nd New York volunteers, Col. P. J. Claassen commanding, and Capt. R. E. Fisk at the company's head.

In the bloody fights that afterward took place this regiment made a record for bravery that stamped it one of the most noted in the whole army, as its comrades of the second brigade, fifth division, 18th army corps, could well testify. Wherever duty called, and the most intrepid feats of courage were required to be displayed, there it was to be found breasting the terrible onslaughts of the desperate enemy. Its many feats of daring challenged the enthusiastic admiration of the gallant foe, and at the same time the envy of its less conspicuous friends. Its post was always where the stoutest hearts and coolest heads and strongest arms were needed; and the brave boys never murmured, always considering that the greater the danger the more glorious the reward. Time and again it crossed bayonets with the enemy in the death struggle, and seldom came out of the frightful struggles with trailing colors. Its front was always menacing, intrepid, invincible, and its advances on the foe like the lightning's flash, and as destructive as the roaring, swelling, sweeping avalanche, or awful mountain flood.

NINE TIMES WOUNDED.

During Gen. RYAN's service with this regiment he was wounded nine times, one of which was very serious, and came near causing his death. It was a hip-joint wound. The ball had to be chisseled out of the bone. He wore it as a charm on his watch chain. Up to the time of this dangerous wound, in February, 1864, he had participated in the first and second battles of Blackwater, West Va.; Suffolk, Va.; the second and third battles at Newbern, N. C.; Little Washington, N. C.; Kingston, N. C.; Pallonksville, N. C., and many others, as appears on the official records in Washington.

PROMOTION.

When in camp at Newbern, N. C., December 1863, young RYAN was promoted to the enviable position of Second Lieutenant of his company. This cheering intelligence was communicated to the gallant young soldier's sister, who was at school in Toronto, Canada, by Capt. "Bob" Fisk, in the following expressive language. After the usual preliminaries, the Captain seems to take delight in saying:

"His papers have been forwarded to Gov. Seymour, of New York. They are signed by his Captain, First Lieutenant, and every enlisted man of the company; and indorsed by Colonel Claassen: *cheerfully approved.* Being in command of the company, I take it upon myself to transmit this most gratifying intelligence to his sister and family. His prospect of further promotion is very bright. It is with happy feelings that I testify to the upright and honorable conduct of your gallant brother. Nothing but intrinsic worth and high military ability could have procured for him his appointment."

The gallant author of this manly tribute to the worth of a brave comrade is still living, away out in the wilds of Montana, editing the *Herald*, at Helena, one of the staunchest Republican journals in the west, and will take pleasure in remembering this extract.

BATTLE OF NEWBERN, N. C.

Special mention is made of this battle, because of its terrific nature, and from the fact that in it Lieut. RYAN played a very prominent part, and nearly lost his life. At one time it was believed he had fallen dead at the head of his men, while breasting the awful storm of shot and shell hurled against his line, and this report was flashed all over the country.

In this fearful conflict the 132nd New York was assigned a most important position ; and it might be said the one where the greatest danger was to be encountered, that of the extreme outpost.

The enemy came down like a whirlwind to to the attack, and swept, for a few moments, everything in their way. The contest was fearful and destructive, and lasted five hours. For a long time victory hung in doubt. At last it perched upon the Union arms, and crowned them with a halo of glory; but at a great sacrifice of life. Never before did the enemy display such courge ; their feats of daring being perfectly herculean. But they all proved abortive, and the heroic fellows had to fall back battered, bleeding and defeated.

SEVERELY WOUNDED.

While the shocking carnage was going on Lieut. RYAN fell dangerously wounded at the head of his company, fiercely contesting the ground over which the Spartan armies met in the murderous shock. Thrice the enemy forced their way over his dead, as it was thought, body, and as often were hurled back, until at last they had to give up the bloody strife.

In this terrible battle Lieut. RYAN was stationed with G company on the most extreme outpost, where it required the coolest heads and most dauntless hearts to do a Spartan duty in holding the enemy at bay. The position was a modern Thermopylae, and he was the Leonidas, with his gallant band, selected to hold the distinguished post of danger and honor. And well and faithfully did he do his duty. His dauntless leadership, and the pre-eminent courageousness of his men, contributed immeasurably in saving the Union arms from a demoralizing defeat. For his heroism he was advanced to the position of First Lieutenant, besides receiving the congratulations of his commanding officers, and the plaudits of the newspapers of the country.

As the crash of battle was dying away, and the smoke of angry guns rolling off from the gory field, our young hero was taken from among the dead and mangled by a few of his intrepid followers and borne to a place of safety among his friends.

For several months his life was despaired of while in hospital at Newbern. At one time it was thought necessary for his life to amputate his leg at the hip joint, a thing he would not tolerate. Finally his great vitality and recuperative powers of body conquered every evil, and bid defiance to death, and he soon returned to duty.

In the meantime he had been removed to

the Ladies' Home Hospital in New York.

HIS GALLANTRY COMMUNICATED TO HIS SISTER.

The bravery of Lieut. RYAN in the defense of Newbern can be better appreciated by a perusal of the subjoined extracts of letters.

Capt. Fisk writes to Miss Ryan:

"*** It gives me infinite pleasure to record that in the late fierce engagement on the outposts at Newbern your brother greatly distinguished himself as a brave, efficient and daring officer. His gallant conduct on the momentous occasion has won for him that high praise and commendation which the true soldier so much covets, and which he often does not hesitate to lay down his life to obtain."

The following is an extract from a letter of Geo. E. Bostwick, of H troop, 12th New York cavalry, to P. Burke, St. Thomas, Ontario, Canada, Lieut. RYAN's uncle. The writer and the subject of the eulogy were school-fellows in their youth, and very much attached to each other:

"* * * When the attack was made Lieut. RYAN was in command of his company, and on the most extreme of the outposts. He gallantly resisted the advance of a heavy body of rebels, and held them in check for five long hours. He was severely wounded, and saved from capture only through the cool, intrepid daring of two of his brave men, who carried him off the field under a scathing fire of the enemy. He is now in the officers' ward of Foster Hospital, Newbern. His conduct in the terrible conflict is spoken of by those who had a good opportunity of knowing as being fearless and heroic. He was everywhere in the thickest of the fight, encouraging his men to deeds of unexampled daring. At one time he severely repulsed several impetuous charges of a whole rebel brigade, and held them in check until he was reinforced, thereby saving our arms from a disastrous defeat. Your nephew is spoken of as the 'bravest of the brave,' and I am proud to be able to tell you so.''

Lieut. RYAN's meritorious acts on this occasion called forth the unbounded applause of the general public. Even the rebel papers spoke of the "dauntless courage displayed by a handful of men in our front, the leader of whom was shot down by our men, but not in time to give us victory.''

TROUBLE AHEAD.

Just so soon as our hero could be removed he was sent to New York. While in the Ladies' Home Hospital there he noticed quite a number of flagrant derelections of duty on the part of some of the officials. These he severely commented upon through the public press. This had the effect of drawing upon him the displeasure of Dr. Mott, the surgeon in charge, who preferred charges against him for conduct detrimental to the service.

A court martial was convened before Capt. John Fritz, of the 93rd Pennsylvania volunteers, as president.

The result of this was the finding of the accused guilty, and his subsequent dismissal from the service, with stoppage of all pay and allowances.

But Mott's revenge was not of protracted duration.

AT HIS GRANDMOTHER'S DEATH BED.

While the preliminaries of the court martial were going on, our hero was suddenly called to the death chamber of his grandmother in Toronto. He applied for, and received leave of absence to attend the solemn occasion, and arrived just in time to see her life flutter into eternity, and receive her parting kiss and blessing.

As the tall, pale, war-worn young soldier entered the darkened chamber, he was immediately recognized by the helpless lady, over whose aged face stole a sweet smile as he reverentially stooped and kissed her pallid lips. His mother and sister were standing by and fondly embraced him, while big tears rolled down their cheeks. As the dying lady

kissed and blessed her gallant nephew, she
feebly said :

"My child, have you your dear grand-
father's medal with you ? "

On it being taken from his breast and presented to her, she kissed it, then muttered a
blessing upon those standing around; a little
sigh followed, and the spirit of the noble old
lady flew to heaven and laid its acts of three
score and six years at the feet of her blessed
Redeemer.   She was buried with Roman
Catholic church rites, and placed in the same
grave between her idolized son and much beloved husband.

HIS CANADIAN RECEPTION.

While in Toronto our hero attracted considerable courteous attention from " our Kanuck
cousins," notwithstanding that the unpleasant shadow of the Trent affair still hung
gloomily about them.   No matter where he
went his bright blue, and gold epauletted uniform and pale face attracted a bevy of joyous
ladies and gentlemen, who left nothing undone to make his short stay in the city of his
birth pleasant.

REFERRING TO PRESIDENT LINCOLN.

On Lieut. RYAN's return to New York the
court martial held its session, with the result

before mentioned. It was a severe blow to the young hero, and aroused the just indignation of his friends.

But he did not despair. Immediately he appealed to Governor Seymour of New York, who at once had the facts laid before President Lincoln, asking a reversal of the action of the court martial.

In this the Governor was ably seconded by Senators Morgan and Harris, and Congressmen Darling and White, and General K. C. Hawkins, all of New York. This action was accompanied by a strong appeal from Col. P. J. Claassen and every officer and enlisted man of the gallant 132nd N. Y.

In support of Lieut. RYAN's cause, and to show at what infamous hands he was suffering, Gen. Hawkins, in a letter to Gen. Dix, said :

"Dr. Mott is a most infernal scoundrel, and I am now obtaining such evidence against him that will astonish everyone."

And in the same letter he continues :

"Lieut. RYAN is a soldier and a gentleman well worthy your most favorable consideration."

DISABILITIES REMOVED.

Upon the representation, by Gov. Seymour and others, of all the points in the case, and they having been carefully reviewed by Judge Advocate General Holt, President Lincoln "*cheerfully removed*" the disabilities referred to, and the soldier who dared to publicly expose the misdeeds of his superiors in rank stepped from under the ignominious cloud they wished to throw over his fair name free and untarnished, and victorious over the miscreants who desired to humble and disgrace him.

MADE A CAPTAIN.

At this time Col. N. G. Axtell was completing the organization of his regiment, the 192nd New York, at Albany. To this meritorious officer Lieut. RYAN was introduced by Col. Geo. A. Buckingham, of the 52nd New York, a gallant soldier. It was such dashing young officers as RYAN that Colonel Axtell wanted, and he gladly appointed him Captain of F company. The regiment was sent to duty as a portion of Hancock's celebrated Veteran Corps.

This promotion occurred a few months prior to the conclusion of the war, which glorious event put a stop to the fast developing military renown of the brave soldier. Many distinguished officers have often been heard to say of him that all was necessary was a good field and a fair opportunity to make him one of the most dazzling lights in the galaxy of great military men.

His loss of military honors by the sudden collapse of war's terrible drama was a great national gain in which he gloried.

THE END OF THE WAR.

When the perfume of the flowers of May, 1865, was being wafted from the icy fields of Vermont to the orange groves of the Gulf, the gloomy pall of desolating war was lifted from the nation and hurled into eternity, while the sun of an undivided Union shone forth· with transcendent glory, throwing its lovely folds over the hideous scars of the bloody strife, and kissing the graves of the heroic and glorious unmonumented dead, who fell that the Union might live.

Four years of blood, and carnage, and misery was enough. Lee, Johnson, Beauregard, Dick Taylor, Price, E. Kirby Smith, Forrest, Early, Longstreet, Ewell and Bragg had struck their colors, and the Confederacy tumbled, to rise no more, and the glorious stars and stripes triumphantly floated over the miserable wreck. It went to its sleep of death upon a gory bed, while the flames of the Rebel capital threw a lurid glare over the ghastly ruins everywhere visible. The terrible strife was over, and the nation sent up a long, fervent prayer to God for His great mercy in crowning the Union arms with victory and glory, and humbling to the earth those who wished to destroy the land.

It was a grand, a glorious victory; but one gained at an enormous cost of blood and treasure.

The rebels were terribly in earnest, and it is only justice to say that never were such herculean efforts made by men fighting in a bad cause; and the mystery is, and always will be, how they held out so long and fought so desperately. To say that they did not fight like Spartans would be doing them a grievous wrong, and materially detracting from the halo of glory that circled our triumphant arms.

SWORD PRESENTATION.

One of the last honors paid to Capt. RYAN before leaving the army was the presentation to him by his company of a magnificent sword, belt, pistol, sash and shoulder-straps. The blade was of the finest Damascus steel, the hilt richly mounted in sivler, and beautifully finished, while the scabbard was of pure German silver, artistically carved. The blade was elegantly chased, and on it finely engraved:

"Presented to Capt. W. A. C. RYAN, by the members of his company, F., 192nd New York Vols., as a slight token of their high appreciation of him. March 28, 1865."

This took place in presence of a large concourse of officers and men, who heartily cheered as the dashing, and battled-scarred young hero proudly buckled on the beautiful weapon and gracefully thanked his admirers for the handsome compliment.

Thus ended the brilliant army career of one who had barely reached his majority; a boy in years, but a full man in experience. A stranger in a strange land he had risen from youth's obscurity to a very enviable position as a military man, and to an exalted place in the estimation of the most influential men of the nation—at the head of the list being the murdered President, Lincoln, and the late Vice-President, Henry Wilson. Mr. Lincoln had no sincerer mourner than the gallant young Captain.

TWO PICTURES.

Before the author there are two pictures of his hero—one in his United States Captain's dress, the other in Cuban attire, with a General's stars adorning his shoulders.

In the first he appears draped in a long blue, single-breasted regulation coat and loose trowsers that set well upon his tall, elegant figure. His fine head is uncovered, and the luxuriant, dark hair cut close. His handsome face is thin, but his very regular features are calm, with the faintest smile playing about his perfectly shaped mouth, while his dark eyes glow with animated fire. A general look of youth pervades his whole make-up, but it is of that jaunty, dashing nature character-istic of the proud, gallant, ambitious soldier who reveres honor and courage.

In the other, taken seven years later, con-siderable change is noticeable. Still there is no mistaking the strikingly handsome face. He is resting in repose, apparently having just dismounted from his horse. He is sit-ting on a log, and withered shrubbery appears scattered around in profusion. His high-booted and spurred legs are stretched out, and across his knees rests his trusty sword. From his waist hang a pair of fine revolvers. His close fitting jacket is thrown carelessly back. A bright star shines on his breast, and three adorn each shoulder. A large som-brero hat rests upon his magnificent head, while a wealth of long, dark, curling hair falls gracefully on his broad shoulders. His fine eyes are cast upon a map, and his beauti-ful lips are tightly compressed, as if in deep study, and a look of anxiety pervades his bronzed face. Fronting on his slouched hat is a little wreath, and inside of it are two crossed swords, in the angles of which is the motto, in initials:

"First New York Cavalry Cuban Liber-ators."

In this likeness his symmetrical figure is fully developed, and he looks the dashing, fearless cavalryman, the dauntless American Murat, the Patriot so loved by the Cubans, and feared and hated by the savage Spanish butchers.

HIS OPINION OF THE GREAT CHARACTERS OF THE AMERICAN REBELLION.

As many will be curious to know General RYAN's estimate of the great lights of the Rebellion, it will not be out of place to say that of the Union military leaders he ranked Gen. McClellan the most scientific, Sherman next, then Grant, McDowell, Mead, Rosecranz, Hancock, Thomas and Sheridan. His admiration for Generals Kilpatrick, T. Francis Meagher, and the late noble martyr, the gay, dashing, fearless, handsome Custer, knew no bounds. And it appears that poor Custer had a high opinion of the Cuban martyr.

Of the Rebels he commenced with Gen. Robert E. Lee, then the dead Albert Sidney and Joseph E. Johnston, Beauregard, Stonewall Jackson, Longstreet, Price, Dick Taylor, J. E. B. Stuart and Forrest, and Arkansas' immortal Irishman, the gallant dead hero, Lieutenant General Pat. Cleburn. Admirals Farragut and Porter were among his idols, and he could not help but admire the rakish rebel rover Semmes. He also held in high esteem the great raider, John Morgan, of Kentucky, and ever deprecated his dastardly murder when a prisoner. Facts in this case he learned from the dashing rebel cavalryman, Col. Geo. Forrester, of Kentucky, who was with Morgan.

Of the civil leaders he lifted the lamented President Lincoln to the most exalted position, but he never failed to acknowledge Mr. Jefferson Davis as possessed of extraordinary abilities. He never allowed the cloud of his treason to obscure his brilliant record in the Mexican war, nor his able services in the national Senate, and as Secretary of War. And his noble heart could not help but beat with sympathy for the distress and misery of the South when her flag was struck and her rebel heart was humbled, bleeding and repentant.

FENIANISM.

It has been a subject of wonder with the general public why Gen. RYAN was not identified with the Fenian movement in 1866, fresh as he was from the smoke and crash of battle, and the cause being so much in need of such able services. The reason is easily told. In the first place, immediately after the war he made business arrangements to go to Montana territory, the breaking of which would heavily involve him, and some friends, pecuniarily ; and in the second place, he believed that the time had not arrived to strke

the blow for Ireland's freedom. He considered that the great barrier to her emancipation from British thraldom existed religiously,
in dissensions between the Roman Catholic
and Protestant churches, and that not until
this black line was erased, and Irishmen could
meet as brothers, united body and soul for
their country's freedom, then, and not until
then might she hope to be free. He considered this clearing away of religious animosi-
ties, aye hatreds, the first grand step to success. Until this was effected he believed all
attempts at throwing off the iron yoke would
be futile and disastrous.

This view he freely expressed to General
McMahon and Colonel Byron, of New York;
Colonel John F. Finnerty and Major W. C.
McClure, of Chicago, and the late Capt. P.
C. Shannon, of Toledo, Ohio, as stanch sons
of old Ireland as ever took an oath to see her
again free and independent, as of yore.

No man more loved the land of his fathers
than General RYAN, and it may be safely said
that he was ready to draw his sword in her
defense when the proper time arrived to strike
down the tyrants trampling upon her dearest
liberties, and he firmly believed that but a
few years would elapse until she could take
her place among the nations of the earth.

BOOK III.

OUT IN THE FAR WEST—MONTANA, ETC.

When the dancing, feasting, and pleasure following victory, and the death of the monster rebellion, were over, and shoulder-straps, gay uniforms, and keen blades were carefully laid aside, as mementoes of the terrible struggle, our hero cast his eyes westward, and determined to try his fortunes in the mines of Montana.

About this time Col. James L. Fisk, before mentioned as one of Capt. RYAN's army comrades, was organizing an expedition to settle in Montana, and was to leave from St. Cloud, Minnesota. RYAN determined to accompany the party, and was gladly enrolled by Col. Fisk, because it was such material as he was made of that was necessary to combat any attack of savages that might be made on the train. The expedition was to start the first of August, 1865.

On account of some negotiations going on between the government and the Indians the expedition was postponed until May, 1866.

NEARLY A FATAL HUNT.

By way of killing time, until the starting of the expedition, which now was to be from

St. Paul, Capt. RYAN and his old army friend, Capt. John W. Fenton, went on a hunting "frolic" into the wilds of Minnesota, during which they experienced terrible sufferings.

One night, in a blinding snow storm, they lost their horses. They were now two hundred miles from civilization. The storm lasted three days, and the weather was very cold. Not a living thing seemed to occupy the desolate waste of ice and snow but themselves and RYAN's splendid Newfoundland dog Monte. The intense cold had frozen the feet of Capt. Fenton, and death stared them in the face. In this shocking situation Capt. Fenton struck on an expedient that proved their salvation. He advised his companion to write a note telling their situation, tie it to the dog's neck and send him out to hunt up friends. This was done, and the faithful animal started on his important mission, apparently knowing what was required of him. He had not been gone five minutes when the stillness of the awful solitude was broken by the sharp crack of a rifle. This was unexpected and startling, and RYAN thought his dog was the victim. Cautiously scanning the wide carpet of snow he detected a stalwart Indian about two hundred yards away, moving at a right angle to his position. Carefully training his rifle he fired, and the child of the forset was sent to other hunting grounds. It was discovered that the savage had shot a fox instead of Monte, much to the joy of Capt. RYAN. The rifle and ammunition of the Indian were taken possession of and the body buried beneath the snow. The fox, a good fat one, afforded food for the two famishing, snow-bound adventurers.

Monte had found friends, and on the fifth day a body of United States Cavalry rescued the unfortunates from a terrible death. But Captain Fenton's feet were so badly frozen that the forepart of them had to be amputated. However, now he walks around Washington apparently unharmed.

The trip was fatal to the faithful dog. The cavalry mistook him for a wolf and shot him, from the effects of which the poor brute died. When the men went to take his "brush" the note was found tied to his collar.

Capt. RYAN was very much grieved at poor Monte's death.

THE EXPEDITION—RYAN NEARLY HANGED.

The expedition left St. Paul on the 5th of May, 1866, and arrived at Helena, Montana, in September. It numbered about 500 men, women and children. The pleasure of the trip was occasionally marred by little skirmishes with Indians, but none were of a serious nature. It was mere amusement for the men, most of whom had smelt powder during the "unpleasantness" between the States.

One incident occurred on the route that came near ending RYAN's days. He was appointed officer of the expedition, and as such enforced army discipline, a fact that made him obnoxious to a few discontented spirits. These became exasperated and formed a plot to effectually get rid of the objectionable character. They were a portion of the men recruited from Missouri and Kansas, and who, it afterward appeared, were ex-members of the Rebel Quantrell's guerilla band of cutthroats. RYAN was made aware of his precarious situation by a young girl who accidentally overheard the murderous scheme. The facts were laid before Colonels James L. and R. E. Fisk, Capt. Fenton, and a few other tried friends, and measures were at once taken to make it hot for the outlaws, should they attempt to carry out their infamous plot. One evening, shortly after the expedition had halted for the night, and while RYAN's trusty friends were scouting around for game, the bandits suddenly pounced upon their intended victim, before he could draw his 'pistol, hurriedly pinioned his arms, ran a rope around his neck, and started for the nearest tree.

While the desperadoes were engaged in these preliminaries, the young heroine before referred to mounted her horse and sped off in search ot the absent friends, while the entire camp was becoming aroused by the startling drama. Fortunately she soon found them.

Then a race for life took place.

In a very few minutes the rescuers arrived, headed by the little Joan of Arc, and just in time to save the condemned, who was calmly standing beneath the limb of a tree, over which was hanging the rope, while the excited camp surged madly around him.

RYAN's friends dashed among the outlaws, pistol in hand, and demanded the cause of the outrage ; and quick as a flash the brave girl leaped from her horse, ran to the prisoner, and in a second severed his bonds with a keen-edged stiletto she drew from the folds of her dress, it and a fine pistol being presents from Capt. RYAN, and the use of which he had taught her.

When free the gallant Captain took his fair preserver's hand, bent low over it, and kissed away its excited tremblings, now that the dread picture was passing away, while the whole camp, save the abashed would-be murderers, set up a prolonged cheer, that swept musically over the wide expanse of uninhabited prairie, and echoed back that the young girl was a true heroine.

It was all that Capt. RYAN and his friends could do to keep the orderly members of the camp from lynching the outlaws, who escaped during the night, leaving a note stating that it was their intention to do away with RYAN, the Fisks and Capt. Fenton, then rob the train and desert.

No, gentle reader, the love between the sweet girl and the dashing young Captain, was only Platonic, and the romance will have to rest there. She was on her way to Helena to marry the object of her heart.

RYAN'S SUCCESS.

Capt. RYAN was among the few of the expedition who were particularly lucky. Somehow fortune smiled on him, and he "struck a streak" that "panned out" well, and soon he was numbered among the wealthy gold, silver and copper property-holders in the territory. The few thousand dollars he brought with him had been invested judiciously, and his pecuniary future looked bright.

On arrival in Helena, Col. "Bob" Fisk and Major Stewart established the *Herald*, the only Republican paper in the territory. The *Gazette*, a rebelized Democratic journal, was "ruling the ranche," and shaping public opinion. Capt. RYAN indirectly associated himself with the Fisk paper, being a stanch Republican.

The political war now commenced in good earnest. But the new paper kept its banner flying in the face of Democratic threats, and bade defiance to the enemies of Republican reform.

In this struggle for a good foothold of the party many personal skirmishes took place between the "young Irish Republican," as our hero was called, and the leaders of the dominant Democracy who had been in the habit of controlling others at the muzzle of a pistol, or the glittering point of the formidable Bowie. In these rencounters he taught the Democratic desperadoes that to "jump his claim" was instant death.

A TRIP TO NEW YORK.

Capt. RYAN's mining property having accumulated so rapidly he determined to go East and dispose of some of it, that he could the better develop the rest.

In May, 1867, he left the golden regions beyond the Rocky Mountains, passed by the grand scenes of the Yellowstone, rested for awhile in lovely Salt Lake City, supped with Brigham Young, floated down the turgid and snaggy Missouri, luxuriated for a day in St. Louis, passed to the Garden City, Chicago, and revelled for an hour in her sumptuous retreats, and had a delightful reunion with his loving mother and sister, the first since the meeting in the death chamber of his grandmother; then a hurried ride to the Empire City, where he sought repose under the sheltering wing of the courteous Leland's in the palatial Metropolitan Hotel, on Broadway.

On his arrival in New York he learned by the papers that his brother J. G. was in Washington, looking after his "false imprisonment case," and had been tangled up in a very-near-shooting difficulty, a not unusual thing where the "wild Arkansan's" rights were trespassed upon. Immediately he telegraphed him at the Kirkwood House, on Pennsylvania avenne—the hotel made famous by being the place where Andrew Johnson was informed that Lincoln had been brutally murdered, and that he was President of the United States—to join him without delay.

The telegram was a surprise to Jack, who answered back O. K. After calling on the President, visiting the Capitol, the Smithsonian Institute, the parks, gardens, Treasury building, and generally "doing" the "city of magnificent distances," including a look at John H. Surrat, then on trial, and a peep at the Old Capitol Prison, that was being demolished, he hastened to New York, where he arrived the evening of June 12th, and was soon enjoying and Arkansas "rooster's narrative"—straight whisky—at the Metropolitan.

On his arrival he learned that W. A. C. would not be in until 11:30 that night, so rambled into Niblo's Gardens to witness the Black Crook, that many-legged drama that became such a target for the moral anathemas of some pulpit orators, who took good care to visit the play, that they might the better expatiate upon its "demoralizing tendencies, and immodest features."

This over, he returned to the pleasures of his room, to await the coming of him he had not seen for many years.

MEETING OF THE BROTHERS.

When the clock had marked that it was nearly twelve, a knock was heard at Jack's door.

"Come," answered he.

At this invitation, in stepped a tall, dashing, splendid-looking young fellow, whose broad-brimmed slouch hat cast a dim shadow over his extremely handsome face.

"Beg pardon, is this Capt. J. G. Ryan's room?" inquired the person.

"It is."

"Can I see him?"

"Certainly, sir; that is, if you will cast your cerulean orbs in the direction of the anatomy standing before you," said our Arkansas traveler holding out his hand. He had recognized Will at first, notwithstanding the many changes of their long separation.

"What!" excitedly exclaimed Will, stepping forward and grasping the extended hand; "is it possible this is you Jack?"

"Fact; all that you Yanks left of me."

It is needless to say that the meeting was affectionate and happy, for the brothers were very dear to each other.

As the surprise was over Jack "rang up" a couple of refreshing juleps, over which they discussed the subject of their long separation, and the many romantic adventures each had passed through.

"Yes, Jack," said Will, "it is twelve years since that gloomy night when you left your mark upon that unfortunate man. And mother still lives with him. Strange! Well, if there ever was a martyr, she is one, and Saint Peter will not hesitate to open the gates of heaven to her when she knocks for admittance. I had the happiness of seeing her and sister in Chicago on my route here. They inquired affectionately for you. I see you have taken after the Burkes in stature. Five feet eight, aye; well, I thought you would have been taller. Sorry you were on the losing side in the late war."

"So am I," chimed in Jack, with a smile that meant he was sorry his side had been so unfortunate.

"Your side made a terrible fight," continued Will. "You must have been fearfully in earnest. The world never before witnessed such heroism."

"Yes," responded Jack, "my people, as you say, were fearfully in earnest. We all were soldiers, both men and boys; and the women, old and young, did a Spartan duty in favor of the cause, and if ever I write a book they shall see justice done their noble deeds."

"What you say of the ladies is true," said Will; "but give up your combustible writing; that *Vindicator* of yours is as bitter as gall and hot as caustic. You must cool off and become reconstructed."

"If I were a profane person I would say recon-h—l," replied Jack. "Why, sir, if you had been treated with one-tenth the harshness our people have by your radical carpet-bag reconstructionists, but more correctly speaking, thieves and scums of christendom, you would start a first-class graveyard every day. We laid down our arms in good faith, and ever since have been trying to get along quietly, but your villainous carpetbaggers will not let us rest. If I had my way I would give his satanic majesty a chance to reconstruct *them.*"

"Don't you speak from personal feeling, because of the ill-treatment that you received while in gloomy prisons, supposed to have been mixed up with the assassination of good President Lincoln?"

"No, sir," replied Jack; "I speak for the whole country."

"Well, we won't quarrel over the matter,"

said Will. "Let us change the subject and have these glasses replenished. I rarely ever touch the second glass, but as this is a rare occasion I will overstep my rule."

The string was again pulled, and soon a son of Ham ushered in the "cool comfort."

"Yes, Jack, I like Montana very much, notwithstanding its rough society. But this will soon wear away. I look forward to the near day when she will be one of the brightest stars in our glorious confederation of states. Her resources are many, and her hidden wealth far beyond one's wildest imagination. Of course the troublesome Indians on her borders will have to be civilized with the bullet, and railroads established, before the territory will amount to much. I do not know how long I will reside there; probably forever. What's your programme? Law and literature, aye. Well such a life would not suit me, unless it could be attended to on horseback. I like not to be housed up. I love the out-door air, bright landscapes, blue skies, sweet flowers and the joyous songs of innocent birds. Youth will soon pass away before the frosts of age, and while sunshine lasts I mean to enjoy it practically, not in imagination as do most of you literary dreamers."

"I would like such a life myself," replied Jack, "but the fortunes of war dispelled my bright picture for the future, and I look forward to nothing but hard toil. Life is all a farce, anyway, and I care not how soon I go down the dark valley."

"Nonsense. my boy; let your motto be *uil desperandum.* Throw trouble over your shoulder, bid defiance to trouble, start out anew, and drink of pleasure's cup whenever the Cyprian goddess smiles. Life is too short to sigh for disappointed hopes. Let it always be with you *dum vivimus vivamus.* 'There are sunny spots where men may dwell.' Pick them out, and let the icy breath of discontent blow in other regions. There is less danger attached to this than in such desperate charges as you Confeds made at Corinth in October, 1862."

"Yes," answered Jack, "it all looks nice on paper."

Thus chatted the boys, and the night had trespassed far into the morning before they retired to rest.

The stay in New York city was short, but pleasant. After the General had effected his financial arrangements satisfactorily, he, Jack and Capt. Dan. W. Fisk, took a trip up the Hudson, and to Niagara Falls, where they tarried a few days as the guests of that elegant gentleman, Col. John Fisk, and his truly attractive family.

BACK TO MONTANA.

June 24th, 1867, the brothers separated,
Will and Capt. Fisk going to Montana, and
Jack taking a pleasure trip down the St. Law-
rence to Montreal. While in Canada he got
up entertainments for the Southern Hospital
Association in New Orleans, his authority
coming from General Dabney H. Maury.
Although his mission was not a pecuniary
success, still he was warmly received, as a
Southerner, by the Canadians. He had the
pleasure of meeting in Montreal, Toronto and
Niagara town, President Davis and family,
and his brothers-in-law Col. " Bill," Jeff.,
and — Howell, Dr. Luke P. Blackburn, of
Kentucky; Hon. John — Mason, of the
steamer Trent affair; Gen. Carroll, of Tenn.;
and many other distinguished Rebels. When
on this mission of charity, Col. Ryan says
that while the churches merely "recommended" the object, the theatrical profession un-
animously gave their services free. This was
notably the case with the Myers troop from
Rochester, N. Y., playing at Toronto. Mr.
Myers, and his beautiful daughter Fiora, being "Yankees," a cheering evidence that
noble hearts still beat in Northern breasts for
their suffering Southern sisters.

En route West General RYAN again had the
pleasure of meeting his loving mother at the
Sherman house, Chicago. The strongest
bonds of affection existed between the parent

and her dear son. She fondly worshipped
her darling, and he returned her love with a
warmth becoming his noble, impetuous nature. No more respectful, obedient, and loving man or boy ever existed, and it is told of
him by his sorrowing mother, that in his
youth he never retired to bed without offering
up prayers to God, and embracing her with
kisses.

AGAIN IN THE GOLD REGIONS.

On Gen. Ryan's return to Helena, he and
Col. W. S. Scribner, late Secretary of Montana under Gov. Thomas Francis Meagher,
and acting Governor after that distinguished
gentleman's sad death, established a much
needed "quartz mining bureau and real
estate agency;" its main object being the
giving of permanent form and intelligent direction to all mining matters. The most
scientific men in the several mineral depart-
ments were employed, and Prof. Aug. Steitz,
of the First National Bank, was engaged as
assayer. In this institution the buyer and
seller had equal facilities for gaining accurate
information. A fine reading room, parlors,
and other attractions made the establishment
the grand bourse of the territory. Among
those who patronized it were Governor Green
Clay Smith, Hon. W. F. Sanders, The First
National Bank, Gen. Neil Howie, Gen. Sol.
Meredith, all of Montana; Hon. James M.

Cavanaugh, Washington, D. C.; U. S. Senator Ira Harris, New York; Gov. Lucius Fairchild, and Hon. Thomas Reynolds, of Wisconsin.

Business poured in from the start, and continued favorable, until the proprietors had made their "pile," and sold out in 1869.

In August, 1868, Gen. RYAN again visited New York, Philadelphia, Boston, and other cities, in the interest of Montana, and disposed of a large quantity of valuable mining property, belonging to himself and others, to good advantage.

FACTS ABOUT GEN. MEAGHER'S DROWNING.

Gen. RYAN and the dashing leader of the gallant Irish Brigade were strong friends, and it will not be out of place to here correct the infamous slander that the illustrious Irish-American was a "drunken suicide." It is a fact that the boat on which was the Governor, while going up the Missouri river, had a portion of her cabin guards knocked away—just in front of the General's stateroom. The was night dark. It being rather warm in the cabin the Governor stepped out on the guard to catch the breeze. It is supposed he never thought of the destroyed railing, and that while he was feeling for it in the gloom he fell overboard and was drowned. His body was never recovered. This statement was made to the author by several gentlemen of Washington, Capt. John W. Fenton, he believes, being one.

And an item to the same effect is found in Gen. RYAN's diary.

RYAN'S MONTANA TROUBLE'S.

By some unlooked for streak of fortune, RYAN and Chas. W. Sears discovered that the finest-built-up section of the city of Helena had not been entered in the land office according to law, and thereupon immediately took steps to "jump" it in their own names. When the occupiers of the property became aware of this fact, their astonishment was great, and can be more easily imagined than described. A meeting of all concerned was held, and the greatest excitement prevailed. Threats were freely made to appeal to Judge Lynch, as the easiest way of settling the matter; and at one time it looked "kinder dark for the boys." Nevertheless, the startling fact stared the property owners square in the face that their valuable improvements belonged to two keen speculators. But notwithstanding their good fortune things looked decidedly blue for the latter. They could not help involuntarily putting their hands to their necks, and jumping up, to see if they were still on terra firma. Finally the matter went into court, and RYAN and Sears came out the victors. But the "hanging" pressure was so great against them that they had to compromise with the original owners, by which they received good titles.

It was generally conceded that if this settlement had not taken place the exasperated people would have coolly and deliberately strung up the obnoxious individuals.

OUTLAWRY.

Prior to 1866 life in Montana was very precarious. Bands of desperadoes infested the mines and raided the settlements, and caused a reign of terror to exist. Horrible murders and highway robberies were of such frequent occurrence that no one considered himself safe. In 1864 these outlaws were banded into an organization called the "Road Agents." They murdered, robbed, and outraged indiscriminately.

Among the most noted of these scoundrels were Henry Plummer, Charley Reeves, —— Moore, and —— Skinner. They took the Montana fever while in Oregon, and at once rushed to the new Eldorado, and pitched their tents in Bannock City. Between there and Virginia City they operated, while their infamous gang daily increased in numbers. At one time it was hard to find an honest man in this region. The outlaws were a regular terror, and none but the stoutest hearts dare dispute their right to do as they pleased. They were splendidly armed, and mounted on the fleetest horses. When they dashed upon the unsuspecting traveler, and shouted from behind their masks:

"Halt, hold up your hands,"

The demand was, it is needless to say, immediately complied with, the party attacked feeling grateful if they spared his life after robbing him.

THE VIGILANTES.

These outrages became so glaring that the good citizens secretly organized themselves into a Vigilance Committee and commenced a war of extermination upon the cut-throats. By the capture and confession of two of the murderers, the names of the whole gang were discovered. These two were Erastus Yager and E. Red, whom the Vigilantes subsequently hung in the Stinking-water Valley. Through these it was learned that the gang numbered fifty.

In six months after the Vigilantes commenced operating the band was entirely broken up, and nearly annihilated.

Of the entire gang J. A. Slade, Henry Plummer, Boone Helm, Geo. Ives, Bill Bunton and Cyrus Skinner, were considered the most blood-thirsty. Their motto was:

"Dead men tell no tales."

They all died with their boots on.

It was not until about 1870 that all of this terrible tribe were extirpated.

RYAN AND PARTISANSHIP.

On account of his strong Republican principles "Whack" RYAN, as he was familiarly called in the mountains, became very obnoxious to the Rebel-Democratic element in Montana, who took every opportunity to cast slurs upon him. But he was always splendidly "heeled," that is, well armed, and ready for "business."

One day a fellow calling himself "Colonel Bill Granger, by Gawd, sir," and believed to have been one of Quantrell's guerillas during the Rabellion, "waltzed" up to him, while he was in conversation with some gentlemen, in Alder Gulch, and commenced using offensive language, with the intention of creating a disturbance, keeping his hand on his pistol all the time. At last he staggered against Whack.

That movement gave a physician a fee.

Quick as a flash RYAN drew his heavy revolver and struck the miscreant a blow that knocked him senseless to the ground, where he lay, until carried off by some miners to a ranche, where his skull was dressed.

Afterward the bully apologized to Whack, who returned him his pistol.

Several other such difficulties elevated our hero considerably in the estimation of the desperadoes. But he had a number of narrow escapes from death.

As to duels, and being engaged as second in affairs of honor, he figured frequently and conspicuously; always coming out of them untarnished for courage, and the justness of his cause.

His most celebrated difficulty was with Geo. M. Pinney, a banker of Helena, and at one time an influential member of the Republican party. This Pinney had the audacity to break open a sealed package deposited in his bank by Gen. RYAN. Because of this base treachery, Whack had him branded as a scoundrel. Pinney tried the intimidation game; but it would not work, and he had to "crawfish" in a very humble manner.

Now, in 1876, this same Pinney is a refugee from justice, having defrauded the United States government out of a large amount of money, and fled the country, a circumstance that sustains Gen. RYAN's assertion that he was a thief and a scoundrel.

Judge May and Colonel W. Woolfelk, of Helena, had a little spat one day. The former not receiving a prompt apology, at once sent a challenge by Whack. At first the Colonel demurred, but finally apologized, sooner than see himself posted around the streets as a coward, scoundrel, and mean paltroon.

Among Montana's "upper crust" the inexorable "code" was the great court of appeals to settle the most trivial infractions of right or honor.

In General RYAN's diary is the following entry, July 6, 1868:

"Pulled Deslock's nose this eve. for his impertinence, and saved Chas. W. Sears' life from being taken by a gambler. I got the 'drop' on him first."

The "drop" means covering the enemy with your pistol before he has time to draw his weapon.

Another entry, July 16, 1868, reads:

"Colonel Chestnut insulted me. I gave him a chance to send a challenge. I accepted it. When on the ground he declined becoming an angel. Glad of it, for he is a fine shot, and I might have went up."

Another:

"July 31, 1868.—Difficulty to-day in court between Col. Woolfalk and Judge Chinsen. The Colonel slapped the Judge in the face, and broke his cane over his head. Judge Munson ordered the Colonel to jail for contempt. No officer would execute the mandate."

These items are introduced to show the

"delightful" state of society in the far West. But such little episodes were scarcely noticed by the denizens of that oriferous region, for nearly every man could point to his private graveyard.

That the reader may not imagine that Gen. RYAN was easily led into these serious difficulties, but acted at all times in self-defense, the following circumstance is introduced, which is one out of thousands:

After the conclusion of the Rebellion, Gen. Martin Beem, of Chicago, whose health had been considerably injured by Rebel bullets, went West to enjoy the revivifying air of the mountains. No more quiet or less aggressive gentleman ever existed. One day, while enjoying a siesta on a rude bench in one of the "hotels" in Virginia City, Montana's late capital, his peace was suddenly interrupted by an uncouth animal belted with heavy pistols and a huge Bowie, who began profanely announcing that he could cut the heart out of any d—d Yankee in the diggings, at the same time driving his knife into the counter and calling to the barkeeper to "dish up some more good licker." After thus stirring up his courage, he commenced indirectly addressing insults to General Beem, whose army record and Republican politics he had learned from the hotel clerk. The General knew that a man's life was not worth much in the estimation of the blackguard, so began to quietly get into position to resist an attack. He had a splendid Smith & Wesson pistol easily accessible. At last the storm commenced, by the ruffian approaching the General in a threatening attitude, with his glittering Bowie held firmly in his hand.

Like the lightning's flash, the feeble General drew his revolver and presented it at the rascal's head, telling him that another step would be his last.

"Stranger," said the miscreant, "you have the age on me; let's compromise and licker. You've got it to say that you're the only man that ever got the drop on Cap. Bledsoe. I'm yer friend hereafter. Shake."

The General considered it politic to shake, but would not "licker," because he never indulged in intoxicating beverages.

This individual was the terror of the mines, and started a graveyard wherever he went.

At last he received his desserts. The brother of one of his victims coolly blew his brains out in Diamond City, without giving him a second's warning.

This was the class of characters General RYAN had mostly to contend with.

FIGHTING SITTING BULL.

As this notorious savage has become so infamously celebrated by his massacre of the gallant General Custer and his noble band, (last June, 1867), it may not be out of place to state that General RYAN fought against him on several occasions. In 1868 Sitting Bull made a number of raids into the white settlements of Montana, and the Governor had to call out volunteers to protect the people. RYAN was one of the first to tender his services. The Indians were defeated in every battle, and nearly annihilated in Gallatin Valley. There they were drawn into an ambush and literally cut to pieces. General RYAN was one of the squad that decoyed the red devils into the vortex of death.

This summary punishment of the savages was at the time strongly censured by a number of Washington peace-policy fogies, and stigmatized as a terrible massacre.

Spirits of the murdered Generals Canby and Custer, and their martyred followers, awake, and call down heaven's lightning upon all such conservers of the peace, that they may be smote into oblivion.

THE U. S. MARSHALSHIP.

When General RYAN returned from his Eastern trip, in the fall of 1868, his friends induced him to become a candidate for the office of United States Marshal of Montana, soon to be vacant by the expiration of Gen. Neil Howie's term. He was considered the most suitable person that the Republicans, as a party, could present to the President for his nomination to the position. No man was better qualified to discharge the onerous and hazardous duties of the office successfully. He possessed all the grand requisites, honesty, integrity, acumen, quick perception, administrative and executive ability, and cool, invincible courage, a thing absolutely necessary to enable an officer to faithfully discharge his duties among desperadoes who cared nothing for life.

However, other parties became candidates, and Gen. Howie intended making an effort to retain his position. In this he was ably backed by the recreant banker Pinney.

AT THE NATIONAL CAPITAL.

When March, 1869, arrived, the time for "log-rolling" had come around, and the several aspirants for the marshalship, and their friends, hurried to Washington. Among those who accompanied General RYAN were Colonels W. S. Scribner, R. E. and James L. Fisk, and Capt. John W. Fenton.

A heavy pressure was brought against Howie by most of the Montana Republican Central Committee, because of his being led by Pinney, whom they denounced to President Grant as unscrupulous and dishonest, and who was manipulating the office of U. S.

marshal for his own venal aggrandizement, and to the detriment of the Republican party.

General RYAN's name went to the President *strongly recommended* by Hon. Green Clay Smith, Governor of Montana; the late Vice-President. Hon. Henry Wilson; United States Senators R. E. Fenton, T. O. Howe, Matt. H. Carpenter, —. J. Robertson, and —. L. Fowler; and by Representatives Gen. B. F. Butler, C. C. Washburne, W. A. Wheeler, now, in 1876, candidate for Vice-President on the Republican ticket; I. Buffington, A. H. Jones, B. F. Hopkins and R. W. Butler. And this extremely flattering array of indorsers was reinforced by the earnest wishes of thousands of Montana's best citizens for his appointment.

General C. S. Hamilton, of Fon du Lac, Wisconsin, threw a destructive shell into the Howie ranks by means of a severe letter to Secretary of War Rollins against Pinney, in which he said :

"Geo. M. Pinney is the wickedest scoundrel West of the Mississippi river, and the deliberate murderer of our friend Governor S. W. Beall, late Lieutenant-Colonel 18th Wisconsin Vols. He is now in Washington endeavoring to regulate the disposal of Montana offices for his own benefit. I hope the murderer will be treated as he deserves."

Senator I. M. Ashley, and Hons. B. P.

Hall, James M. Annity, W. A. Jones and C. H. Ball, also threw their influence in favor of RYAN.

And the late Vice-President, Henry Wilson, sent Attorney General Hoar a strong letter urging his " young friend's " appointment. The distinguished statesman had a great liking for General RYAN, and this was fully reciprocated by him. General RYAN's admiration for his illustrious patron was so great that he presented him with a beautiful and magnificent cane, curiously wrought, and specially manufactured for the purpose, at considerable cost. No doubt this souvenir is still in ·Mr. Wilson's family. The autograph letter accepting it is in the keeping of Col. J. G. Ryan.

During the hot canvass for the marshalship Geo. G. Huntingdon, of New York, took up the gauntlet for his thievish friend Pinney, and savagely assailed Gen. RYAN by letter. The General replied that if he came in his way he would treat him as he had Pinney and his hired assassins, and denounced him as a contemptible puppy.

Mr. Huntingdon took good care not to cross the General's path.

The feeling was so strong in favor of Gen. RYAN for marshal that Col. Thos. Cottman, a very prominent candidate, gracefully hauled down his colors and espoused the cause of the former.

"All's well that ends well."

TREACHERY.

Gen. RYAN was cosily seated in his room in the Metropolitan, on Pennsylvania avenue, when a waiter presented a card.

"My friend Fenton," he murmured, as he read the card. "Show him up."

"How are you Whack?" cheerfully said his visitor as he stepped in.

"Splendid, Captain," replied Whack. "Be seated, John, and try some of this wine. Don't be afraid of it, it is splendid. Would not a little of it have been a God-send when we were lost in that terrible snow-storm in Minnesota?"

"It would, indeed. It is really fine."

"What's the news, John?"

"Confounded bad, Whack, if it be true."

"What is it; anything going wrong about the marshalship?"

"Yes; I have just learned that your supposed friend, the Judge, has turned traitor, withdrawn his name from your papers, and deserted to the enemy."

"Is it possible," ejaculated Whack. "If there are traitors in camp we must hunt them down. Let us go to the Attorney General's office and find out. By the eternal, if the report be true, that old miscreant shall never be a United States Judge of that territory. I will 'rob him of his expected bliss,' as the song goes."

They jumped into a carriage, and were soon at the Attorney General's office.

There General RYAN learned that the report was only too true. The ·Judge, whose name the author regrets he does not know, not only withdrew his name, but gave as a reason that the General was *not* qualified for the position.

This set RYAN in a white heat of passion.

Into the carriage again, and down to the Metropolitan hotel.

When in his room, General RYAN said to Captain Fenton:

"John, scratch out a strong doucument for that contemptible fellow to sign, *retracting* his assertion as to my competency for the office my friends wish to elevate me to. Put it in language that would bring a blush to an honorable face. Make it hot as Indian whisky."

"Probably he won't sign it, Whack?"

"Sign it!" said our hero, sarcastically. "Yes, he will, John, or I'll die trying to make him."

The paper was drawn up as desired, and no man was better qualified for such a task than its author. This accomplished, both

o

put on some "artillery," in case "business"
would require it, and then sallied forth in direction of the Capitol, where the Judge was
wire-pulling for the position to which he as-
pired.

NEARLY A COW-HIDING MATINEE.

On their way to the Capitol General RYAN
purchased a substantial raw-hide, which he
secreted up his sleeve.

Capt. Fenton knew what this meant, and
began to cogitate on the probable result. He
knew if the Judge failed to sign the document the General would unmercifully casti-
gate him.

The Judge was found in one of the Senate
cloak rooms.

General RYAN walked up to him, and said:

"Judge, I am informed by the Attorney
General that you, sir, have withdrawn your
name from my papers, giving as a reason that
I am not qualified for the position, etc. Now,
sir, believing you were forced to take this
disgraceful step by the Pinney faction, I
brought this instrument for you to sign. You
will perceive it is addressed to the Attorney
General."

The Judge took the document, and hurriedly perused it. As he did so the color
went and came to his face. At last he looked
up and said:

" Ryan, I can't sign this."

Giving him one of those cool, calm, penetrating looks from eyes of burning lightning, the General responded:

"You won't, eh? Well, we'll see about it," at the same moment quickly drawing the whip. " I guess you will sign it."

Nervously, the Judge continued, as he gazed on the instrument of torture, and remembered in what determined hands it was :

"Well, Ryan, I am getting into deep water in this matter."

"So you are," replied Whack; "and if you do not immediately sign that paper you will find that it is devilish hot, too."

Overcome with fear of his relentless antagonist, the Judge signed the paper, and thereby acknowledged his own infamy.

In a few minutes more it was in the hands of the astonished Attorney General, who, upon reading it, indignantly said :

"A man with no more firmness, self-respect and honor is not fit to be a judge of a United States court," and thereupon requested the President to withdraw the recreant's name from before the Senate, which was done, and the Judge's official hopes were scattered to the winds.

This turn of affairs made Ryan's opponents very bitter, and serious personal results were shadowed, which caused both the RYAN and Pinney factions considerable uneasiness.

Matters looking so grave, the President concluded it best for the interests of the Republican party in Montana to ignore General RYAN, and the other candidates, so nominated Col. W. F. Wheeler, of Ohio, who was confirmed to the position.

MEETING THE CUBAN GEN. GOICOURIA.

During the marshalship excitement, Gen. RYAN met, at Williard's, the celebrated Cuban patriot, General Goicouria, and learned from that aged gentleman's lips the distressing tale of his country's wrongs.

This touched our hero's sympathetic heart, and fanned into a blazing fire the embers of his great martial spirit.

The result was he determined to espouse the cause of Cuba Libre, and risk the perils of a "black flag" war to see her free from the yoke of tyrant Spain.

This determination was strongly opposed by many of his friends, who drew a faithful picture of the horrors he would have to pass through, with a good prospect of meeting the sad fate that eventually placed him upon the roll of glorious martyrs.

But this was all to no purpose. His mind was made up, and the subject possessed him body and soul.

This was the grand turning point in his life, and he entered upon the rugged path that led into the dark valley of death with as light a step and as cheerful a heart as ever characterized the knights of old, who rode forth through their castle gates, battle-ax in hand, to enter the lists against base tyrants.

BACK TO MONTANA.

After concluding to join the Cubans in their struggle for freedom, General RYAN made a hurried trip to Montana for the purpose of settling up his business. This satisfactorily done, he bid adieu to his friends, and made as hurried a return to New York, to enter upon a career that rivalled the most glowing romance, and ended so tragically.

—o—

BOOK IV.

GEN. RYAN AND CUBA.

On his return to New York, in May, he immediately entered into communication with the Cuban Junta, and the several prominent leaders, among whom was General Thomas Jordan, who was, during the late Rebellion in the United States, chief of staff of the

Rebel General Beauregard, and who drew
upon himself considerable Southern odium by
some severe strictures he made upon Jefferson Davis, in *Harper's Weekly*, after the
war.

As soon as Gen. RYAN was duly initiated
into the secrets of the Cuban party he learned
that important work was to be done, and that
General Jordan was organizing an expedition of men and arms to land on the island of
Cuba. Also that General Goicouria was in-
augurating measures for an expedition on a
very large scale, to follow that of General
Jordan.

General RYAN was assigned to duty to assist General Jordan, and when the latter had
his arrangements completed he was entrusted
with the organization of the Goicouria expedition, that created so much excitement in
June and July, 1869, and which was known
as "Colonel Whack RYAN's Gardiners' Island Expedition."

Leaving our hero for awhile, wrapped up
in plans for the emancipation of suffering Cuba
from Spanish thraldom, we will advert to
the war on the "ever faithful isle," and what
produced it.

THE CAUSE OF THE WAR, AND ITS PROGRESS.

According to the best information, no people could have been more loyal than were

the Cubans to Spain up to the year 1820, to which time she enjoyed perfect immunity from the wrongs afterward inflicted upon her, and under which she now, in 1876, writhes in agony.

In 1825 the island was placed under martial law, and a Captain General appointed to rule the "Gem of the Antilles" as he saw fit. The Cubans soon found out that they were considered as mere vassals by the mother country, and had no rights she was bound to respect, and that heavy taxation, without representation, was to be their lot.

This the native, or Creole, element could not brook; but as they became indignant, proportionately the more harsh became their treatment. Down to the most trivial official position, every one was filled by a Spaniard, and the poor Cubans soon found that they had quartered upon them a most disreputable and mercenary horde of foreigners to support, and be insulted by. In a word, every indignity was heaped upon them.

The pressure becoming so frightfully galling they determined upon an effort to free themselves from the crushing yoke.

At last an armed outbreak proclaimed the hatred of the people for the tyrant oppressor. But it was a feeble effort, and soon crushed, at considerable cost to the "rioters," as the revolutionists were called.

After this outbreaks became of frequent occurrence until the memorable uprising of
the 10th of October, 1868, which precipitated
the horrible war that has been waging ever
since.

The most notable of these was that of the
gallant Lopez and the brave Quitman and
Crittenden, in 1857, the failure of which, and
the sad fate of these leaders, every one is
aware.

THE UPRISING AT YARA, OCT. 10, 1868.

In July, 1868, Carlos Manuel Cespedes and
Francisco Aguilera, residents of Bayamo,
considered that the plans of the revolutionists for a grand uprising were sufficiently ma-
tured for action, but the Junta at Puerto
Principe insisted on postponing the outbreak
for a year, which was agreed to. But circumstances willed it otherwise, and the present bloody strife was commenced.

By treachery, or otherwise, the Spanish
government heard of the purposed revolution,
and sent orders to the Governor of Bayamo
to arrest and imprison a number of persons,
among whom were Cespedes and Aguilera.

This information soon reached these gentlemen, through a reliable source.

Immediately thereafter, on the 10th of
October, 1868, Cespedes and a few followers
captured the little town of Yara, unfurled

the flag of the prospective Republic, and proclaimed to the world that Cuba belonged to Cubans, and that slavery was abolished on the lovely island.

At this time Spain was struggling with a local war of huge dimensions, which subsequently drove Isabella and Amadeus from the throne and raised a Republic, that was in turn soon overthrown, and the monarchy reestablished, with Alfonso as King.

The rebellion of her immensely rich colony somewhat startled the fossilized mother, and she immediately took steps to stamp out the treason. But all her efforts have proven abortive, and the black flag still floats whenever Cuban and Spaniard meet in the terrible struggle of death.

THE WAR.

When news of the uprising at Yara was heralded throughout the island all the patriotic young men of Havana, Puerto Principe, Santiago, and other places, rallied under the bright flag of liberty and swore to be free.

With his white volunteers, and his own liberated slaves, Carlos Manuel Cespedes, the hero of Yara, marched on Bayamo, which surrendered immediately, the garrison not being strong enough to hold it.

There Cespedes established his headquarters, and a provisional government was organized.

Now the revolution began to spread like the wind, and soon the whole Eastern and most of the Central portions of the island were in possession of the exultant Insurgents. The feeble loyal garrisons could not hold out against the impetuous Cubans, and one after another evacuated or surrendered.

By January, 1869, the Insurgents had possession of over half of the island, which is only 700 miles long and from 65 to 260 wide.

At this date Lesurdi was the Captain General. This officer was aware, through experience, that raw, undisciplined men, promiscuously armed with crude weapons, are no match for regular troops; consequently, determined to hurl a heavy force against the Insurgents and at one blow crush the rebellion. But in this he signally failed.

In time he was deposed, and Dulce was placed in command. The latter was soon laid on the shelf, and DeRodas was afforded an opportunity to distinguished himself. Soon his head feel into the basket, also, and Valmaseda was put in his shoes.

Thus change after change took place, but no material advantage was gained over the rebels.

During this time the Cubans who sympathized with the revolution underwent untold sufferings. Women, children, and defence-less old men, were massacred upon the least provocation by the fiendish Spanish element known as the Volunteers.

On one occasion, during a theatrical enter- , tainment at the town of Villanuva a large paty of these scoundrels commenced indis-criminately firing upon the audience, killing and wounding nearly one hundred.

Wherever the Volunteers had power they made a horrible hell of the surroundings.

Captain General Valmaseda, at one time became so disgusted at the horrifying acts o the brutal barbarians that he offered a gen-eral amnesty to the rebels to lay down their arms, that the revolting drama of blood might end. But the Insurgents preferred to suffer rather than return to the fold they so much abhorred.

As soon as practicable after the sudden in-auguration of the revolution the Insurgents established a government similar to that of the United States, and immediately passed an act setting the negroes free. Carlos M. Cespedes was elected the first President.

Of course this humane policy of liberating the slaves strengthened the new cause, and every day hundreds of them rallied under the flag that offered them freedom.

These dusky sons of toil, General RYAN

was very often heard to say; made splendid soldiers.

The choice of Cespedes was a good one. He was in every way qualified for the position; being an able lawyer, very intellectual, of commanding presence, undoubted courage, quick to plan and execute, and a man whose heart and soul was wholly wrapped up in his country's cause.

THE FIRST BATTLE.

After the capture of Yara, Bayamo and Baire, the first victory of importance that saluted the "red, white and blue single-star" flag was in the capture of Jiguani, a town of some pretensions. After a stubborn defence the Spanish flag went down, and the gallant General Marmol marched into the place victorious. This was on the 15th of October, 1868.

In quick succession followed the victories of Caney and Cobre, and the disastrous defeat of the Spanish General Quiras at the head of 4,000 men.

In December, 1868, General Valmaseda, at the head of a large force, swept down on Bayamo, with the intention of capturing the Insurgent government, but his mission failed. He found only the smoking ruins of the rebel capital. The Insurgents had not force enough to defend the town, so made a hasty retreat, removing everything of value, and were well out of danger ere the destroying flames devoured the once happy place.

Now Gen. Valmaseda again offered pacific terms, and a meeting was agreed upon.

But this was prevented by the murder of the Cuban General Augustus Arango, while bearing a flag of truce. As he approached the Spanish lines they coolly and deliberately shot him down, murdered him like a dog while bearing an emblem of peace that the most barbarous and blood-thirsty always respect.

This inhuman act fired anew the Cuban heart, and caused hundreds to rally under her flag that otherwise might have remained in their luxurious homes, far remote from the horrors of the awful struggle.

A most remarkable incident may here be mentioned, and one that seems beyond belief. Two years subsequent to the murder of Gen. Arango, another brother, also a General, deserted the Cuban cause, and went over to the enemy.

The most charitable construction that some have placed upon this act is that he went over to the enemy with the covert purpose of discovering the assassins of his brother, and wreaking upon them a terrible vengeance.

In April, 1869, the Insurgent government located at Guaimara, and a permanent organization took place, with Cespedes at its head, Francisco Aguilera Vice-President and acting Secretary of State ; Pedro Figuerdo Secretary of War, and General Manuel Quesada Commander-in-Chief of the Army.

The Cuban Congress had among its members lawyers, doctors, editors, photographers, school-teachers, dentists, merchants, planters, bankers, etc., but all men of education, and proud of their families and lovers of their country, and terribly in earnest to see her free from Spain's hated control.

In December, 1869, the Spanish force on the island amounted to 60,000, not including 50,000 merciless Volunteers. Besides this large force on land, the island was surrounded by a fleet of twenty-six men of war and eleven gunboats, two of which were formidable iron-clads.

Notwithstanding this immense power of the Spaniards, and the shocking barbarities sanctioned by such human devils as DeRodas, the rebellion prospered, and now still exists in this Centennial year, 1876.

In the latter part of January, 1870, another attempt was made against the Insurgent capital. The Spanish General Puello, a dashing cavalier, started on his raid, with 3,000 well equipped men, to annihilate the rebels. But General Jordan knocked all his calculations into pieces, by suddenly pouncing upon him in a narrow defile, and so utterly demoralizing him that he had to beat a hasty retreat, leaving several hundred dead and wounded behind.

This was one of the most successful battles of the war, and added considerably to the high military reputation of Gen. Jordan.

This was the first battle in which our hero shed Spanish blood. Of it more will be said in another place.

GEN. THOMAS JORDAN.

Here it may be well to state that the gallant General Jordan arrived in Cuba in May, 1869. His expedition consisted of 300 men, and a large quantity of munitions of war and army stores. He landed in the bay of Nipe from the steamer Perrit, where he was joined by 200 new Cuban patriots. While on his way to army headquarters he was attacked by a force of the enemy, which he drove off with considerable loss. On reaching headquarters he was warmly received by General Quesada, and himself and men splendidly feted.

When Gen. RYAN arrived General Jordan took him on his staff, as its chief, then made him Inspector General, and afterward had Congress to make him a Brigadier General and commander of all the Cavalry, a splendid corps of which he, Gen. RYAN, had organized. General Jordan thought a great deal of his young friend, who reciprocated the feeling of his able commander. An extensive correspondence from General Jordan to our hero was found among the latter's papers, and of such a nature as would go to prove that the former had full confidence in Gen. RYAN.

We will now return to New York and take up the regular thread of our narrative.

THE PERRIT EXPEDITION.

After Gen. RYAN had been assigned the duty of assisting General Jordan with his expedition circumstances transpired that threatened the success of the venture. By some unknown means the Spanish Consul at New York became aware that the Cubans were about to send succor to their friends on the island. In consequence of this it was determined, in a conference between Generals Goicouria, Jordon, Cisneros, and Senors Jose Morales Lemus, President of the Junta in New York, Jose Mora, Francisco Fesser, — Alfaro, Dr. Bassora, RYAN, and others, to get Jordan off at once.

This was accordingly done, with the success before stated.

RYAN'S EXPEDITION.

It was now resolved, as Gen. Jordan had gotten off safely. to commence organizing a large force, say a thousand or fifteen hundred men, and a great quantity of arms and ammunition.

To accomplish this the more secretly, and as Gen. RYAN was not known to be identified with the Cuban cause, it was concluded best for him to get up an excitement advising young men to accompany him to Montana to work in his mines. By this plan it was believed adventurous spirits could be reached. And especially when it became known that their expenses would be defrayed.

Accordingly the "man with the white hat," as the New York *World* used to call our hero, because of the immense white slouch hat he affected, opened an office, and flooded the country with circulars.

In the meantime he took into his confidence Col. James T. Clancy, of Boston, a dashing young Irish-American soldier of the Charley O'Malley type, and Capt. A. T. S. Anderson, as fine a fellow as ever professed friendship. To these he entrusted the most important duties of his "emigration" scheme; the gist of which was to discover if the applicant was of a warlike turn of mind, and to select all of such class, and swear them into the League. These, in turn, were used as agents to drum up other recruits. In this manner the work was soon accomplished very satisfactorily, and by June 12th, 1869, over 1,200 picked men were enrolled.

While Gen. RYAN was rapidly performing his part Gen. Goicouria and Senors Altaro, Gonzales and Lemus were actively getting together the war material and army stores, and securing suitable vessels to do the transporting of the men, munitions, and supplies.

General RYAN's part had been performed not only to the satisfaction but also to the admiration of the Junta. His 1,200 "emigrants" had been carefully selected from over 5,000 applicants. Among those chosen were 100 Federal and ex-Confederate officers, comprising two Major Generals, three Brigadier Generals, thirteen Colonels, nine Lieutenant-Colonels, five Majors, and forty-nine Captains and other officers. Of the latter twenty-seven were Prussian, French, and English officers of ability and war experience.

The men were quartered at points so contiguous to each other that concentration was an easy matter.

Everything was working to a charm, and the hearts of all beat high with the hope of soon being on the island striking a heavy blow for freedom.

It was decided that the expedition should leave on June 20th, 1869.

TREACHERY—ARRESTS.

When the sky seemed very clear and bright clouds began to gather thick and dark over the horizon of our hero's new venture, and the bright picture he and his friends had been conjuring up for months was soon to be smeared over by disappointment.

A traitor was in camp, and although he did not know much, still the information he gave the authorities caused the arrest of Gen. RYAN, Colonel Chas. Currier, Dr. Bassora, and Senors Alfaro, Mora, Lemus, Fesser, P. Gonzales, and others, and their indictment by the United States Grand Jury for violating the neutrality laws.

This occurred on the 16th of June, 1869.

IN LUDLOW STREET JAIL.

All were immediately placed in Ludlow Street Jail until they could give bail.

On the 17th of June they were released on heavy bonds.

Now it was determined to immediately get the expedition off at all hazards.

At this critical moment another, and the most fatal drawback occurred. The principal boat engaged accidentally injured some of her machinery, and had to go into dock for repairs.

This proved a terrible disaster.

The calamity caused a delay of several days, and ultimately the failure of the grandest expedition, both of men and arms ever before or since organized for the same noble cause.

On June 22nd, just as the repairs on the boat were finished, and every preparation made to start the next night, Gen. RYAN and those mentioned before, and Col. J. C. Conant, F. J. McNulty and E. A. DeBose, were again arrested and imprisoned.

This time it was charged that the parties on bond had violated their obligations to the law by again acting in behalf of the Cubans, while the other three were arrested on the same charge of violating the neutrality laws.

Public curiosity now became aroused, and the long newspaper articles stirred up considerable excitement in favor of the prisoners, and especially our hero, who was so well known in the Empire City.

After laying in jail all night, they were next day, June 23rd, arraigned before U. S. Commissioner Osborn. District Attorney Pierrepont, now Minister to England, assisted by Mr. Bell, appeared for the State, and Messrs. Sedgwick and Lowry for the prisoners. Col. J. C. Conant, F. J. McNulty and E. A. DeBose were first called, and admitted to bail in sums of $5,000 each.

Here a hitch was discovered in the proceedings, as related to the other prisoners. It was deemed proper to arraign them before Judge Blatchford for acquital or commitment.

At this juncture a good deal of confusion and excitement prevailed among the audience, which was of a very respectable class, and well sprinkled with lovely ladies, relatives and friends of the prisoners.

After considerable deliberation Judge Blatchford concluded to admit the accused to bail in $2,500 each, *except* in the case of Gen. RYAN, which was placed at the extraordinary sum of $10,000.

When this was announced a loud murmur of indignation swept through the court room and flushed the faces of all there, save the Spanish officials and their horde of rascally spies, who seemed supremely happy at the serious situation of our hero.

The fact of this excessive bond goes a long way to prove that the Spaniards must have made out a very strong case against Gen. RYAN, and that the court could not have been pecuniarily prejudiced against him, as many thought.

What a mercenary Spaniard won't stoop to for the accomplishment of his base ends remains among the undiscovered curiosities of this earth.

General RYAN was the leading spirit in this great movement in favor of Cuban independence, and to trammel his actions and thwart his plans in that direction was the one single purpose of Cuba's enemies. And they had at their beck and call the most plastic tools, ready at all times to swear to any monstrous falsehood.

Of course Spain's legal brains in New York, such as the ponderous Sidney Webster, cared little who perjured himself, or who was injured thereby, so their cause was successful and satisfactory.

The glitter and jingle of Spanish gold has a magic influence in soothing troubled consciences, and driving away clouds from the callous hearts of those who reflect not that He who died on the Cross will revise their earthly records.

When the Judge's decision became a fixed fact, Colonel Cummings, of the New York *Sun*, and other friends, stepped forward, and after shaking hands with RYAN, offered to make his bond. This the General would not permit them to do, much to their apparent astonishment.

THE LOVELY INCOGNITO.

At this moment a slight stir was visible in the court room, and a magnificently-formed young lady, richly dressed in velvet, laces and jewels, laid her exquisite hand upon the handsome young prisoner's arm. As he

turned in answer to the soft pressure, her
half-drawn, coquetish veil, disclosed a face of
wondrous beauty. A bright smile wreathed
the cherry mouth, and the fire of pleasure
sparkled in her lustrous dark eyes. The picture was grand, and even attracted the admiration of the serene Judge, who mentally
wished he was in the dashing "filibuster's"
place for awhile. And could he be blamed.
The man who wouldn't risk his second chance
of salvation for a few moments of happiness
in the electrical embrace of such loveliness,
should forever be hurled into oblivion.

What was such an angel doing in that hall
where justice seldom entered?

As the gay cavalier bent low over the delicate hand resting confidingly in his, her
sweet lips parted over the most beautiful of
teeth as she proclaimed in whispers that she
came to go on his bond.

A hurried conversation followed in an in-
audible voice; then in a louder key the prisoner said:

"You have my deepest gratitude, but I
will not consent to your noble wishes. I in-
tend to appeal from the decision of the court
in the matter of this really excessive bond."

As this was said, a close observer could
have detected a meaning look shining in the
radiant beauty's laughing eyes; an expression that plainly said: I understand.

Then the fair vision vanished through the gaping crowd, and excited hearts heaved many sighs that the delicious picture had left them forever.

In a short time after General RYAN refused to be liberated on bail the court adjourned, and he was ordered back to prison, and placed in charge of Deputy United States Marshal Downey.

THE DARING ESCAPE.

Now we have to record one of the boldest deeds ever enacted in daylight, and on such a public thoroughfare as Broadway.

As the Marshal and his prisoner stepped into a carriage, the General remarked to his guardian :

"Marshal, a number of my friends are going to have a jolly time at the Metropolitan, and I would like to be with them for an hour. Let us go up and join them. I know we will have fun."

Marshal Downey could see no harm in such a step, and gave his consent.

The driver was instructed, and off dashed the party. In a few minutes they stopped in front of the hotel, and our hero and his escort where soon in the midst of a gay party who were discussing the Cuban question and matters of the recent arrests.

The company was assembled in one of the

luxurious parlors of that palatial hotel. The assassinated Col. Jim Fisk, and the murdered Mansfield Walworth were there, and Doctor "Buchu" Helmbold, the Fenian Col. Byron, General McMahon, Col. G. R. A. Ricketts, a mumber of newspaper men, the Lelands, and other prominent citizens. It was, indeed, a joyous throng.

Who would have dreamed then that in a few short years four of them would be mouldering in the ground, three having been brutally murdered—Fisk, Walworth and RYAN— and the fourth, the intellectual and splendid Carpenter, of the New York press, the only one dying a natural death.

When the now notorious prisoner stepped into the sumptuous room a loud huzzah welcomed his coming, and glasses were emptied of their sparkling contents to his long life and the success of the cause of suffering Cuba.

After an hour of the most exquisite enjoyment, General RYAN shook hands with his friends, and then told the obliging and much pleased officer that he was at his service.

The two then walked from the hotel and through the immense crowd gathered in front of it to get a look at the soon-to-be more famous prisoner.

From the outside of the great human mass a voice shouted:

"Here's your carriage, Colonel. This

way, sir. Clear the road there, boys, for the Colonel.''

In the direction of the voice the Marshal and his prisoner pushed their way.

The excitement was intense and the crowd cheered lustily.

Now came the startling feature.

As the objects of attention reached the outskirts of the surging mass a carriage drove up and out stepped a deeply veiled lady who was soon lost to view.

At the same instant a cloth was thrown over the Marshal's head, his hands bound behind his back, and himself hurried off, to where he knew not.

Then Gen. RYAN jumped into the carriage from which the veiled lady had disappeared, and throwing a fifty dollar bill to the kidnappers, said:

'' Boys, treat him well, he has been very kind to me.''

Then waving his white hat to the crowd he gave the word and away flew the horses in the direction of Fifth avenue, and were soon out of view.

As the carriage dashed off the crowd gave three loud and prolonged cheers, few knowing the real state of affairs ; but mostly all thinking that the dashing Colonel was on bail.

This was not to be wondered at, as the crowd that immediately surrounded the Marshal and his prisoner consisted of two hundred of Gen. RYAN's "Montana emigrants," assembled for the occasion, and who played their part so well that those outside of the secret ring knew nothing of what was going on.

When the secret at last leaked out, and search was instituted for the missing Marshal, then, in earnest, the excitement became universal, and the garbled accounts of the escape in the evening prints were digested with avidity in every section.

Marshal Barlow was one of the last to hear of the astonishing affair, and the mysterious whereabouts of his unfortunate deputy. But the latter was safe and unharmed, and in due time was returned to liberty.

Marshal Barlow set all the police machinery in motion for the apprehension of Gen. RYAN. But all his efforts were fruitless, and it is safe to presume that as his crime was only civilly criminal those sent in search of him did not trouble themselves very much to find out his whereabouts.

Among the Spanish authorities the excitement was very great, and their calm, satisfied air of the morning had given way to one of fear in the evening. They rushed around frantically, and offered large rewards for the

General's capture. But their efforts were all in vain. He was safe beyond their reach.

THE SECRET RETREAT.

When Gen. RYAN jumped into the carriage it whirled off in the direction of Central Park. At the corner of 25th street and Fifth avenue it halted, when its occupant, now in the garb of a "granger," stepped out and strolled leisurely in the direction of the Fifth Avenue Hotel. Near it a private carriage was drawn up. Into it the "granger" stepped, and was driven to an elegant cottage near Central Park.

In a few minutes he found himself comfortably seated in a splendid parlor, chatting gaily over a glass of wine, with our court-room divinity of the morning, another lovely creature, and General Goicouria, Captain Anderson, and Senors Lemus and Alfaro.

All had a good laugh at the expense of the zealous Spanish officials, and heartily rejoiced that their own plot had been so successful.

The two ladies present were the main agents in making the escape such a decided success over the base intentions of the enemies of Cuba.

They were both brunettes, and of the same style of beauty, each being bewitchingly lovely and youthful. One was a Cuban by birth, and the other a Creole, and a native of

New Orleans. And both were thoroughly wrapped up in the Cuban cause.

It was the New Orleans beauty who played the part of driver of the first carriage Gen. RYAN entered when escaping from the Marshal; and the Cuban "queen" that of the one in which he appeared as a granger, she having left the first carriage as the veiled lady, and then quickly changing her attire in the Metropolitan, hurried to the rendezvous near the Fifth Avenue Hotel.

THE NEW ORLEANS BEAUTY.

It would not be politic to give the names of these heroines, but as a sad romance attached to the lovely creature from New Orleans, and which was the subsequent cause of her lending her aid to the Cubans, it may be of interest to relate it.

She was the only daughter of a wealthy Louisiana planter, whom we will style Col. Borreo. He joined hands with the Confederacy, and feel with the "lost cause" a total financial wreck. Then he removed to St. Louis, where he borrowed a large sum of money from a private banker named Cash. This he soon lost in speculation. During this period Mr. Cash became a visitor at the residence of the Colonel, and was much attracted toward his daughter, the lovely and accomplished Octavia. This soon turned into entrancing love. One day he made known his passion to the Colonel, and asked permission to address the object of his adoration. The Colonel offered no objection, but mentally said, "of course she will not countenance him."

But the sequel will tell.

When the Colonel's consent was received Mr. Cash drew from his pocket a receipt for $50,000 which he handed to the former, saying:

"My dear friend, this is a present; your notes I destroyed this morning. If I succeed with your lovely daughter you shall have a check for $25,000. I will call on her to-morrow. Good morning."

He was gone before the bewildered man had time to recover from his trance-like astonishment at this unheard of freak of good fortune.

During this interview the bewitching girl was reading Ivanhoe in an adjoining parlor, and unintentionally overheard what transpired.

Her young heart had not yet been pierced by the arrows of other than parental love, and it still ached from the wounds caused by her much beloved mother's death, and her fond father's misfortunes.

"Twenty-five thousand dollars," she murmured. "Twenty-five thousand dollars for

my consent to an unnatural marriage! This
sum would once more place my dear father
outside the toils of want and misery. I will
consent; I will marry him; but will not be
his wife. I shall never sleep in his embrace.
I liked the man as my father's friend; now I
abhor him. But I will make the sacrifice for
my poor father's sake."

And she did make it.

Next day Mr. Cash offered his heart, hand
and wealth to his new-made idol. She took
the subject under advisement, and in three
weeks accepted his offer.

The same day the Colonel's word was good
for $25,000, and the future looked bright.

On giving her consent, Miss Octavia insisted upon a quiet marriage, and an exten
sive tour.

In due time the nuptials were performed.
The bride and groom were in traveling dress,
and everything ready for the trip.

While receiving the congratulations of a
few friends, Mr. Cash was summoned to
repair to the Lindell Hotel immediately, upon
" life or death " business, as the note read.

This was a ruse of the wily beauty.

While her husband of a few minutes was
gone, she fled from her father's home forever.

Her plans and disguises were so well ar-
ranged that she experienced no trouble in

reaching New York, where she had one true school friend.

She mailed a little note, before she left, telling her sorrowing father not to look for her, that search would be futile.

This the heart-broken man never disclosed to the frantic and half-crazed husband.

Every artifice was resorted to, and all the brains of the detective department used, to discover the bride of an hour, but all to no purpose.

Finally the wretched father and distracted husband went to New Orleans in hopes of finding her secreted among the friends of her youth.

Fatal trip. While there Yellow Jack cast his poisonous breath upon the city, and hurried into unexpected graves hundreds of old and young.

Among the dead were Colonel Borreo and Mr. Cash. They took sick in the City Hotel, and died there, notwithstanding the care of the proprietor, Colonel Morse, and the skill of the best physicians.

This shocking news reached the virgin widow through an advertisement published by the cashier of her husband's bank, desiring her presence.

When the affairs of her husband and father were settled up she found herself heir to two hundred thousand dollars in cash.

With this large sum she returned to New York and took up permanent residence with the friend of her youth, the lovely Cuban, whose aged parents had to flee from their elegant island home to escape the horrors of Spanish thraldom.

Being of a very sympathetic nature, it was but a short time until she became thoroughly wrapped up in the Cuban cause, and from that hour her heart, soul, energies and money were sacrificed on the altar of her independence. And when death suddenly, in 1873— a few days before the murder of our hero— summoned her to heaven, the cause suffered a great loss, and drew tears of sorrow from hundreds of hearts that had witnessed death in the most hideous forms; and hands roughened by the toils of bloody war smoothed the earth on her peaceful grave, and placed sweet flowers on the marble that marked the young heroine's last resting place.

Her close association with the Cuban cause threw our hero and herself together; and his bold and fearless stand for the freedom of the people she so much loved, drew her to him in the strongest bonds of *friendship*. And the tender feeling was nothing more than purest friendship. No doubt this declaration will disappoint the romantic reader, who would, no doubt, like to have read that the fascinating girl and the handsome young warrior had stepped together into the glorious

web weaved by Hymen. If any deeper affection germed in their hearts no record was
left, save what might have been wafted to
angels' bowers on sweet zephyrs' wings.

THE SECRET COUNCIL.

To return to the secret retreat of General
RYAN, where we left him delightfully situ-
ated with the two young beauties, the distin-
guished General Goicouria, the dashing Capt.
Anderson, and the stanch patriots Lemus and
Alfaro.

The ladies had doffed their male attire,
and nature's loveliness looked exquisitely
adorned as they reclined on rich velvet sofas
draped in costly and enchanting fabrics.

As the party laughed and chatted, Colonel
Arthur Brocarde was announced.

Upon entering the room he gallantly
saluted the ladies, and congratulated the
company on the happy occasion. Then gave
General RYAN a telegram he had received for
him from Col. Geo. R. A. Ricketts.

The General tore it open, and discovered
that it was from his brother Jack, who was
at Memphis, en route from Pine Bluff, Arkansas, to join the Cuban cause.

The situation being so grave, the General
concluded to telegraph him not to come. By
the time this telegram reached Jack at the
Peabody Hotel, Memphis, the papers of that

city had the news of the General's arrest.

Upon the receipt of the telegram Colonel J. G. about faced, and returned to his law and editorial labors in that State where an editor must introduce himselt to a community by making and angel of one of its citizens; and where a lawyer's library consists of a dilapidated digest and a splendid double-barrel shot-gun.

At this council of leaders, which was reinforced by the presence of that noble and patriotic lady, Madame Villaverde, than whom no truer heart ever throbbed for her outraged country, it was decided, at the suggestion of Senor Alfaro, to get the expedition off the night of June 26th, as everything was in readiness.

Before the council broke up, General RYAN scratched off the following note to United States Marshal Barlow, which appeared in the New York *Herald.* It was written at eight o'clock at night, June 23, 1869. It reads :

"GEN. BARLOW—I deem it an act of justice to inform you that Deputy Marshal Downey discharged his duty faithfully; that it was impossible for him to help himself when made a prisoner by my friends, as he was bound hand and foot, and promised a 'gag' if he attempted to call for assistance. I very much regret having been compelled to this step, but I think the act was justifiable. I assure you that he has very comfortable quarters, and was handled very gently. I have no hesitation in telling you that it was my intention to respect my bonds, and that every word in the complaint against me is false."

It was upon the affidavit of a traitor named St. John that all the rearrests were made.

THE SPANISH CONSUL.

After the first flush of excitement attending the miraculous, dare-devil, Claude Duvaul escape of General RYAN had passed off, the Spanish Consul held a council of war, composed of his legal adviser and his horde of spies, and determined upon a vigorous effort to capture the "filibuster," as they called him. This failed, so far as their main intention went, but resulted in the rearrest of Col. Currier, and the confinement of Capt. James Peters, Col. Clancey, and Col. V. Michaelovsky, a Polish-Cuban, supposed to have been accessories in the great escape. They were placed under heavy bonds by Commissioner Shields.

Col. Currier was treated shamefully, being kept in irons most of the time he remained in prison before his release on bail.

It is a fact much to be regretted that some of these Spanish spies were ex-Federal officers. And it was a subject of wonder with those cognizant of the disgraceful fact how they could have stooped to acts so very degrading.

These miscreants would forge letters of introduction from prominent gentlemen recommending them to Gen. RYAN as persons qualified to make good recruits for his "emigration" expedition. But our hero was always on the alert, and had his scheme so well guarded that all such attempts to penetrate his secret failed. Even the traitor St. John knew nothing positive, and the arrests made on his information were with the hope that something tangible would leak out during the investigations.

THE GARDINERS ISLAND EXPEDITION.

The night of June the 26th, 1869, was a very memorable one in the annals of the Cubans and their friends in New York.

It came on like a big cloud, and enveloped the city in a pall of blackness, cheerless and threatening to behold. Then followed crashing thunder, sweeping winds, and flaming lightning, while the rain came down as if heaven's flood-gates had been opened and the waters turned loose upon the earth. It was an awful night, and disastrous for the poor Cubans.

Before the terrific storm broke loose in its awful fury, an interesting scene was to be witnessed at Elm Park, Staten Island. There beneath the gathering storm were assembled 500 so-called Montana emigrants. In their midst stood their leader, tall, erect and proud, with his dark-blue cloak thrown carelessly back, and his broad-brimmed white hat turned jauntingly up on one side, allowing the flickering light of the camp-fires to kiss his handsome face. He was addressing them a few patriotic remarks, reminding them of the great undertaking before them, and that they must nerve their hearts to meet the issue.

As the stimulating words fell from his lips, and were borne afar on the roaring winds, a loud shout of applause rose high above the coming storm that plainly told what implicit confidence those bold spirits had in him under whose banner they had rallied for freedom's cause.

At other points more men were awaiting the order to move.

ON BOARD THE STEAMER CHASE.

Just as the storm broke forth in terrific fury, General RYAN and his adventurous followers had embarked on the steamer Chase which was to take them to the steamer Catherine Whiting, chartered to land the expedition on Cuban soil.

For hours they cruised about in the fearful

darkness, which was only relieved by the winged lightning as it flamed through the heavens, and disclosed for a second the foam-capped waves of the angry waters as they tossed the vessel high in the air, and then let it fall deep down in the turbulent sea, in search of the Whiting, but found her not.

At last daylight appeared, and with it came the news, delivered by a friendly tug-boat, that the Whiting had been captured by the revenue-cutter McCulloch.

It is natural to presume that nothing but base treachery caused the Whiting's capture, a calamity shadowing the failure of the splendidly appointed expedition.

The storm still raging in wildest fury, and another vessel being necessary to fill the place of the Whiting, Gen. RYAN concluded it the best plan to land on Gardiners Island, down the Sound.

This was done, and the men made as comfortable as possible.

Then the steamer Cool was chartered, and sent to New London, Connecticut, for provisions, and other necessaries.

Fortune still frowned. The Cool, like the Whiting, feel into the hands of the revenue officers, and was embargoed at Fort Hamilton, under the menace of its guns.

This serious state of affairs was rather trying on the " boys," but the cheerful spirits of their leader drove away the gloom as the fearful storm slowly spent its destroying wrath.

The only shadow that rested upon the men was the fact that the enterprise was about to fail, and that the " First New York Cavalry Cuban Liberators " would be scattered forever. And this cloud became darker when the news was received that the other detachments of the expedition had been captured, and were under arrest.

Up to July the 4th, things were gradually assuming graver proportions. News was received from the city that it was impossible to charter a vessel to take the expedition, as ship owners dreaded the fate of the Whiting and Cool, and that disbandonment was evident, because of the energetic movements of the United States authorities to capture Gen. RYAN and his faithful followers.

When the morning of the 4th dawned the last ration in the commissary department was gone, and the messenger sent up to New York city for supplies had not arrived. Knowing the day before that such would be the case, Gen. RYAN, to keep up a proper *morale*, had an order issued for the men to be in line by six o'clock in the morning to salute the great national day.

The programme worked well, and the at-

tention of the men was thereby easily drawn
from their aching stomachs to the patriotic
orator dilating in florid speech upon the glory
and greatness of the American Union.

But this unction did not suit quite a number of the auditors, who could not help looking from the grand pictures drawn by the enthusiastic speakers to the very questionable
one presented by the undue exertions of some
of the government's officials to prevent succor reaching a people endeavoring to strike
off the tyrant's chains and become a free and
independent republic.

Gen. Ryan was deeply wrapped up in such
reflections when a tug-boat arrived with provisions, etc.

Among the stores was a barrel of good
whisky. Some of this the General had immediately issued to the men, and soon all
were as "happy as clams."

One of the party, a loquacious, pretentious,
presumptuous son of the Emerald Isle, having taken an extra "tod," asked permission
to make a speech about his much oppressed
country. He professed to be very "larned,"
and was, indeed, quite polished; but when
least expected the mask would fall from his
"iligant" manners and disclose the hideous
defects he tried to hide.

Of course the General granted permission,
and Professor de O'Rafferty mounted an old

box, and commenced his oration by smoothly saying:

"Fellow-soldiers—You must pardon my introduction of Greek and Latin phrases, which I will translate as I proceed. They will be necessary to fully illustrate the glories of the classical ground over which I will have to chaperone you in my remarks. Being fresh in scholastic ethics I feel that I can speak the more understandingly upon a sub-· ject that should interest every true patriot."

This neat exordium elicited great applause, and satisfied the audience that the "Greek and Latin phrases" would be no detriment to the interest of the address.

When the applause subsided, the Professor entered upon his subject in true oratorical style, and for twenty minutes passed over some of the most luxuriant and interesting landscapes of his country's history.

But now the "little dhrops" he had been moistening his mouth with as he proceeded began to operate, and he soon fell from the sublime to the ridiculous. He suddenly left the grave of Robert Emmet and commenced to descant on the:

"Iligant go-ats, the fragrant geese, the melojus swines, the angelic donkeys, the grand mountains, the majestic valleys, the sumptyis whishkee; all these prove injubitably that she is one the gratest kunthries undther the broad kannippy of hevven, it is; and I can proov it, I can."

Then quickly wetting his lips with a little more of the "crather" he raised his voice and emphatically concluded:

"And be jabers, any man that says to the conthrary are *liards* and *scabs*, they ar."

This extrordinary translation of the Greek and Latin phrases of the speaker started the humor of his audience, which broke forth in the loudest peals of prolonged laughter.

The Professor had scarcely ended his address before some unforseen power upset his equilebrium, and laid him out for the balance of the morning.

This little episode added materially to the pleasures of the day, and it is presumable that years elapsed before Prof. de O'Rafferty and his Greek and Latin phrases were forgotten by some of those present.

THE ORDER TO DISBAND.

Affairs on Gardiners Island remained monotonous and uncertain as to the future of the expedition until the 18th of July, 1869.

On the morning of that day General RYAN received an order from Senor Aliaro to immediately disband his men, and to go himself to Canada and await orders; that Marshal Barlow was making a descent on the Island,

and all would be certainly captured and imprisoned.

This order was delivered by Captain Anderson, who urged the General to obey it at once.

There was no alternative left but to obey this command of the Junta.

When everything was in readiness to disband, Gen. RYAN made a short speech to the men regreting the painful course forced upon him, and parting from them with profoundest sorrow.

After the address the men were again sworn to secrecy and fidelity, and the command formally disbanded, after the few hundred dollars borrowed from Mr. Gardiner were equally divided.

Then Gen. RYAN and Colonel Currier took their departure, and were not heard of until the reached Niagara Falls on the Canadian shore.

It is merely justice to say that Mr. Gardiner and his family were extremely kind to Gen. RYAN and his men during their stay on his island, which lasted twenty-two days.

It was Gen. Goicouria's orderly who betrayed the mission of the Catherine Whiting, thereby blasting the hopes of General RYAN in his venture that cost so much money and valuable time.

How hideous is treason.

THE BARLOW RAID.

Gen. RYAN had scarcely been lost sight of, and before the boat had arrived to take the officers and men to New York, when United States Marshal Borlow's anticipated raiding party arrived on the U. S. revenue cutter Mahoning, Capt. Webster commanding, and Lieut. Simms in charge of the marines.

Colonel Arthur Brocarde and Capt. A. R. Rapp were left in command of the men, until they evacuated the island.

Of course the "capture" was an easy one, and Gen. Barlow's celebrated "campaign of the Hackensack" was shorn of some of its glory by the failure to capture the "notorious filibuster chief."

As no war-like materials were found with the "emigrants" they were released when they reached New York.

It was said that Capt. Webster treated Capt. Rapp shamefully, while Lieut. Simms was very courteous to every one coming under his jurisdiction.

Thus ended General RYAN's first blow for Cuba's freedom.

GEN. RYAN IN CANADA.

When Gen. RYAN arrived in Canada he and Col. Currier made the Clifton House, at the Falls, their headquarters, where their presence attracted considerable attention; partly because of the General's extraordinary escape from the U. S. Marshal.

While at the Falls a number of plans were laid to abduct him to the American side, that he might be turned over to the tender mercies of the enemies of Cuba, and be treated as the Spaniards might dictate.

But they all failed.

One of the parties to these attempts at kidnapping was named James H. Day. He had by some subtle means ingratiated himself into the General's good graces. Through this fellow's agency the Spaniards thought they could get the man they hated into their power once more.

That somebody came to grief the sequel will tell.

COWHIDING DAY.

Through the agency of Capt. Anderson, Colonel Arthur Brocarde, and Captain J. C. Harris, Gen. RYAN was informed that Day and others were endeavoring to lessen him in the estimation of some of his lady friends in the Empire City, besides conspiring with the Spaniards for his capture. The slanders perpetrated by this miscreant and his confederates were of the most infamous character, and richly merited the punishment that was inflicted upon Day.

On the 7th of August, 1869, Day visited General RYAN at his hotel, and was invited to his rooms, where quite a number of gentlemen were gathered, all well acquainted with his scoundrelly conduct, and aware of what was in store for him.

When he unsuspectingly entered the room and extended his hand, the General grasped it firmly with his right, and with his left dealt him a ponderous blow square on his face that felled him to the floor and brought the blood in a stream from his nose. Some of the blood the General caught in a goblet, and with it made the unfortunate man sign his name to one of the Clifton House letter-heads.

When this had been done, General RYAN gave the wretch such a sound cowhiding that he got down on his knees and begged for mercy.

After the castigation Day wrote, over *his signature in blood*, a full retraction of his cowardly slanders. This document was witnessed by Mr. A. Wenton, the telegraph operator at the hotel, and immediately sent to the New York *Herald*, and published.

The remarkable paper is now in the possession of Col. J. G. Ryan, the General's brother.

Another of the defamers received a similar horse-whipping on the public thoroughfare of

Broadway, in front of the Stevens House, October 9th, 1869.

Some may consider Day's punishment very great, but let all such reflect, and remember the rascally part played by that individual in attempting to destroy the character and trammel the liberty of one who had been his friend when clouds hung dark and threatening over him. A person less cool than Gen. RYAN might have rewarded such treachery with a bullet, the argument used in Texas.

It is a very easy matter to smear ink on a white fabric, but a work of labor to remove it effectually.

The slanderer is an abomination that should find no shelter in the sanctum of honor, and ought to be abhorred and frowned upon by all lovers of virtue.

RETURN TO NEW YORK.

It was not until Sept., 1869, that General RYAN effected a compromise by which he could return to the United States.

This clemency was accorded by President Grant, upon Marshal Downey promising not to prosecute the General for having him so unceremoniously spirited away in June.

It is said that on the General's return to New York he met Marshal Downey on the corner of Chambers and Broadway, and after a hearty hand-shaking, that they adjourned to Delmonico's and laughed and chatted over the Marshal's startling adventure while sipping delicious wine, and conversed very freely upon Cuban matters.

The Marshal asked the General pointedly why he had not given bail, instead of going through so much romance.

"Simply because," said the General, "I had my plans so well laid to get off the expedition that such a thing as failure did not seem possible, and I was determined to go. If I had allowed my friends to make the extremely heavy bond I could not have gone on my mission without seriously involving them. Consequently, I plotted to escape, and would now be in Cuba if it were not for the betrayal of the Catherine Whiting."

"What has it cost me, and what reward do I expect?" continued the General. "I will tell you, Marshal. So far my connection with the Cuban cause has cost me not less than $20,000; and this does not include the heavy cost of the arms seized from my friend Pond, up the street, for which I gave my paper; nor $9,000 I borrowed from my other stanch friend Geo. R. A. Rickets, the President of the American Bureau of Mines, which went into my betrayed expedition. As to recompense for my time and money, I ask only a share in the glory following the independence of the island, and a recognition commensurate with my services when the emoluments are being awarded.''

''And you have a hope that Cuba will be able to throw off the yoke of Spain? ''

''Not a hope, Marshal, but a firm belief in the success of her fight. I may not live to see that glorious day, for the fortunes of war are treacherous, but it will come ere many years have been rolled into eternity.''

''I judge by your remarks that you purpose going to the island and drawing your sword against Cuba's foes?''

''Yes, Marshal, and as soon as possible. Remember, this is *sub rosa*,'' answered the General; whereupon they separated.

The Marshal was destined to again figure in the General's arrest.

PLOT TO BLOW UP THE SPANISH GUNBOATS.

It will appear strange to the reader, when the memory is refreshed, that while the United States government was thwarting General RYAN's plans, and in every manner throwing mountainous obstacles in poor Cuba's way, she was materially aiding Spain by permitting her to construct ships of war in her docks, and purchase large supplies of war materials from her private arsenals. But such is the fact known to the whole world, and very much wondered at by political philosophers from one end to the other of the civilized world.

While these efforts were being made by the courts of Messrs. Osborn, Shields and Blatchford, aided by Marshal Barlow, and a host of spies fed by Spanish gold, the latter nation was having rapidly constructed thirty gunboats in New York harbor to operate against the friends of the land she was ruling with ferocious despotism.

This fact irritated some of the friends of the "ever faithful isle" to such a degree that they determined upon an effort to prevent them from reaching their destination.

After due deliberation it was resolved to blow them up by means of torpedoes, and every arrangement was perfected to carry out the terrible design, whenever the boats were on their way down the bay to the ocean.

The eventful hour at last arrived.

The night of December 21st, 1869, was announced by chilling winds and glittering stars, and the bustle and noise attending the exit of the gunboats. The fine Spanish war vessel Pizzaro, that was to convoy the new boats to the sea, was vomiting forth a thick mass of blackest smoke, and moving restlessly at her moorings, while the decks of her thirty "chickens" were alive with seamen running rapidly hither and thither completing arrangements for their departure.

While this was going on, two tug-boats might have been seen quietly steaming down the bay close together. When they arrived at a certain point they slackened steam, held a hurried council, and then silently eased off from each other, while at the same time paying out a lengthy cable.

Along this cable, at short intervals, were strung countless formidable torpedoes made principally of that terror of an explosive, nitro-glicerin.

This chain of death was stretched across the track to be followed by the Pizzaro and her thirty young relatives.

The plan was, that so soon as the Pizzaro's prow touched the cable the tug boats were to slacken a little and slightly drop to her stern until the whole convoy was inside the annihilating cordon, when the rope was to be let go and allowed to drift under the vessels. Then the electric current was to be turned on, the missiles exploded, and the victims sent flying into the air.

About nine o'clock, amid loud cheers from some, and hoots from others of those gathered on the wharves to see the vessels leave, the magnificent Pizzaro weighed anchor, fired a salute, and proudly steamed away, followed by the objectionable boats.

In a few minutes the nose of the leading vessel touched the awful line, and the hearts of those in the secret thrilled with hope at thought of the horrible drama about to be enacted.

Gradually the blood-chilling tragedy was approaching.

A few seconds more and a terrific roar would startle the country, fill the air with fire and smoke, and strew the waters with mangled forms and shattered timbers.

But this frightful picture was not allowed to startle the world.

More treachery had taken place.

Just as the the electric current was about to hurl so much destruction into the Spanish vessels, a streaming rocket was seen to shoot into the heavens and burst over the bay.

What did it mean?

Simply that those engines of war should be allowed to proceed unharmed on their mission to plunder, outrage and murder poor, suffering Cubans.

Why was this step taken at the very last moment?

The plot was the work of Gen. RYAN and a few of his trusty Gardiners Island braves.

In the secret was General S. P. Spears.

Designedly, or otherwise, this person made the members of the Cuban Junta aware of the terrible nature of the project two hours before the fatal spark was to have illumined the bay with the fire of death.

Immediately the President of the Junta hastened to General RYAN and implored him to countermand his orders, that the destruction of the boats in American waters would militate against the cause, and in any event would be productive of little good. This plea was so strongly urged that the General consented, and the "danger" signal went flaming into the clouds just in time to prevent the commission of one of the most daring deeds ever evolved from the brain of lion-hearted man.

It will be seen that had Gen. Spears preserved the secret of the plot, a blow would have been struck for Cuba that would have fully compensated for the failure of the Gardiners Island expedition.

This interference of the Junta with the acts of Gen. RYAN caused him to make a newspaper war upon some of its members whom he considered incompetent to discharge the duties of the offices they held.

These newspaper articles produced a reorganization of the Junta, and placed Senor Aldama at its head, the person advocated by Gen. RYAN, because of his immense wealth and presumed fitness for the position.

But the future convinced the General that he was mistaken in his high estimate of Mr.

Aldama's qualifications for the important position to which he was elevated.

When some of the facts relating to this plot became known the New York press in the interest of the Spaniards gave all sorts of highly-colored versions of the affair, and it was not until Gen. RYAN published a letter in the Charleston, South Carolina, *Republican,* a few days after its failure, while on his way to Cuba, that the country became aware of all the facts necessary to exonerate the Junta from blame in the desperate venture, he assuming all responsibility.

OFF FOR CUBA, AT LAST.

The prospect being rather gloomy for getting off anything like a large expedition, because of the strict surveillance kept by the United States authorities over the movements of suspected Cuban sympathisers, and petty jealousies having arisen between the friends of the cause in New York, on account of Senor Aldama's elevation to the Presidency of the Junta, Gen. RYAN and a few friends, Cubans and Americans, determined to run the gauntlet themselves, and go to the " gem of the Antilles."

Accordingly they chartered the fleet steam yacht Anna for the occasion. She was commanded by Capt. Rudolph Sommers, and had a crew of nineteen.

The night of December 29th, 1869, the little vessel, with her select passengers stowed snugly away, silently slipped out into the broad ocean, and started on her perilous mission to the Gulf.

Captain Sommers was not aware, at the time his vessel was chartered, of the "character" of his passengers, who numbered only twenty-two, and whose "baggage" was very heavy.

Soon, however, he was enlightened, and an offer made to him for the purchase of his vessel. This was accepted, and one of the "passengers" took command of her.

The weather being exceedingly rough, the vessel was forced to seek shelter in Charleston harbor for several days.

When the storm abated the Anna was run in among the Bahama islands, where she met the brig T. Field of New York, in charge of Albert A. Fernandez, with a cargo of arms, munitions of war, and army supplies. This was soon transferred to the Anna, and at 5 o'clock in the evening of January the 14th, 1870, she steered for Cuba, under a high head of steam.

This cargo consisted of a large number of Springfield and Remington rifles, Whitney and Colt's navy revolvers, machettes, and sabres; a great quantity of caps and cartridges, and rifle and cannon powder; two twelve pound howitzers, medicines, clothing, stationery, printing materials, etc.

The mysterious " passengers " of the swift and rakish little Anna, consisted of General RYAN, Gen. Cisneros, Dr. C. Emilio Mola, Colonel James F. Clancy, Captain Tom Lile Mercer, Capt. Ricardo Ponce de Leon, Capt. Oscar Cespedes, Eloy Camachs, Melcher Aguera, Carlos Mayar, Rafael Cardova, Julien Campaniera, A. M. Rojas, Vastie Autie, Angel Fomes, Juan Luis Ariasa, A. Eschemardia, Juan Rius, Isidora Portillo, John Williamson, and others.

SAFE ARRIVAL.

The evening of Jan. 19th, 1870, the Anna, with steam off, lights out, and but little sail flying, cautiously stole into the beautiful bay of Neuvitas.

The night was very propitious for landing, being quite cloudy, but the air was as mild as a Northern June, and richly laden with perfume of sweetest flowers.

What a change! When the party left New York the ground was sprinkled with snow and the breeze cold and biting ; here it was spread with a carpet of green, birds sang and twittered gaily in the trees, and the air came freighted with delicious fragrance.

The cargo was soon safely on shore, the artillery placed in position, sentinels and pickets posted, and every other precaution taken to resist an attack.

Then a courier was dispatched to apprise the nearest post of friends of the successful landing.

Having satisfactorily accomplished her mission, the gallant Anna, after being sold back to her former owner, turned her head Northward and was soon lost in the distance, as she went quickly bounding over the frothy billows.

On reaching Nassau the little craft was betrayed by one James Rogers, her steward, into the hands of the United authorities on a charge of having violated the neutrality laws, and detained for several months.

IN CUBA.

The following hurried letter from General RYAN to his brother Col. J. G., at Pine Bluff, Arkansas, will be found interesting, coming as it did fresh from the land of horrible war and hideous desolation.

It was written in camp near Neuvitas, Jan. 19th, 1870. It reads:

"DEAR BROTHER—Here I am at last on the 'ever faithful isle,' but would not be if fortune had been less kind. I have only a few minutes to write. It is now midnight, and the Anna leaves in an hour. Our party left

New York the night of Dec. 29, 1869. The
weather being very severe, we had to run
into Charleston for safety. There our papers
were overhauled. If we happened to have
had any suspicious 'baggage' on board, off
would have went our heads. As it was, considerable skirmishing was necessary to save
us. While in that port I met some splendid
Southerners, of ex-rebel proclivities like your-
self, and was treated well by all. Besides
them, I had the pleasure of meeting several
United States officials, all whole-souled gentlemen, and Cuban sympathizers. Among
them are Lieut. Keene, U. S. revenue, Major
J. E. Patterson, Col. W. L. M. Burger, Capt.
John Townley, Col. T. N. Warner, General
James Totten, Col. J. W. Nicholls, Captain
Stone, and several beautiful and accomplished
women. (I mean the ladies first.) I enjoyed their princely hospitality fully. There
is something about this Southern country so
genial that one seems drawn to the people in
a way pleasurable beyond expression. You
know I prefer sunshine to clouds, consequently I drink deep of social pleasure whenever opportunity offers. Shortly after leaving Charleston we ran in among the Bahama
Islands, where we met the brig T. Field,
Capt. Emerson. From her we received our
war materials, which have been safely landed
here on the margin of the beautiful bay of
Neuvitas. We are right between two Spanish

forts, and all around rise into the sky masts
of their war vessels. Things are ticklish.
However, we are prepared for a fight. Col.
Clancy would consider it a great favor to be
afforded an opportunity to try his pop-guns.
Every minute I expect a body of our friends
to arrive to escort us to headquarters. ᐧ This
is a lovely night, only a little cloudy. What
an extreme change a few days have made.
When we left New York it was bitter winter,
here it is delightful summer. Well, I must
now say adieu, for Capt. Sommers is ready
to start. I will write again soon, if I don't
lose my scalp. Affectionately,
" W. A. C. R."

In a few hours after this letter was written
the expected escort arrived, and the expeditionists started for army headquarters.

THE FIRST BATTLE.

When Gen. RYAN reached headquarters he
found Gen. Jordan starting on his expedition
to intercept the advance of the celebrated
Spanish Gen. Puello, who was dashing to his
doom at the head of 3,000 well disciplined
cavalry.

Immediately upon becoming aware of this
movement Gen. RYAN volunteered to take
part in the battle, and the gallant General
Jordan accepted his services as one of his
staff.

As before stated, the hopes of Puello were suddenly blasted when Jordan and his braves dashed down upon him like a sweeping avalanche, and utterly routed his forces.

Gen. RYAN's dare-devil courage in this glorious victory won him a bright place in the hearts of his comrades that he held forever after during the many terrible conflicts they together participated in.

FIRST IMPRESSIONS.

The subjoined letter of General RYAN to his brother will give a good idea of how he was impressed by affairs in the Insurgent district. It was written a few days after the Puello defeat, in camp near San Miguel. It will be found very interesting:

" * * * My reception at headquarters was quite complimentary. Generals Jordan, "Bembetta" and F. Varona, Vincente Garcia, Modesto Diaz, C. A. Acosta, Ruvalcaba, and Colonels M. E. Aguera, L. C. Bailey and James Rooney, and Gen. Diaz's wife and several other lovely ladies were present, and gave me a cheering welcome. All around camp were scattered groups of soldiers, in every conceivable costume; and some with scarcely any garment on. These kept a respectful distance, but looked curiously at me. Under your ex-rebel General Jordan's fine discipline these men resemble old veterans.

Negroes and whites fraternized quite Democratically, and appeared one homogeneous family, a sight very strange.   *   *   The people must be terribly in earnest, or they never would have stepped out from their homes of luxury and elegance to accept a life of extreme hardships and gaunt poverty. That they are determined to be free from Spanish thraldom can be seen in their every action ; and very sensibly felt in the flashing of the black eyes of the beautiful women in tattered garments.   I can now partly realize how fearfully in earnest you rebels were in our late war.   This one here is about a parallel case.   The Cubans are surrounded by the black ruins of their once happy homes. Their palatial mansions, elegant garments, and sumptuous fare, have all disappeared. But amid this awful desolation they stand proud, defiant, unconquerable ; determined to sink into martyrs' graves sooner than return to the hated embrace of the poisonous fold they had left.   *   *   *   Americans are favorites with the people ; and especially is this the case as to Gen. Thomas Jordan who, ere long, no doubt, will be commander-in-chief of the army.   I am anxious to meet my old United States army friend Gen. Frederic Cavada, and expect to in a few days.   He holds an important command.   *   *   Gen. Diaz wants me on his staff, as do others of the prominent Generals ; but I shall remain with General Jordan. He is going to have organized a select Cavalry corps, and has entrusted to me the important duty of perfecting it. When the organization is complete I am to be its commander. * * * Jack, if I do not fall a victim to Spanish bullets, I am afraid I will to one of these beautiful Cuban girls. Some of them are exquisitely lovely, and most charming in their ingenuous ways. As I write, one of the bewitching creatures is sitting, a short distance off, playing on a guitar, and singing a martial air. Her voice is rich and full, and its melody steals over my soul like ——. Confound the luck, why wasn't I created a poet, so I could picture my entrancing feelings. The fact is, I must cease writing, and get closer to that magic voice. WHACK."

"P. S.—I came near forgetting to tell you that we everlastingly whipped the enemy the other day. Gen. Jordan was in command, and covered himself and men with imperishable glory. WILL."

FROM GEN. RYAN'S DIARY.

The following items are taken from the Journal of General RYAN, and will be found quite readable:

"Jan. 30, 1870.—Gen. Jordan very ill, from effects of over-exertion in the recent battles.—Mr. Goosman just arrived with a

message from President Cespedes. Mr. G.
has presented me with a magnificent stallion
never ridden.—This a. m. I wandered over
the battle-field of the 27th inst. Dead Spaniards, horses and mules are scattered around
in numbers, fed upon by buzzards, and pois-
oning the air with a disgusting stench. It
was a lively fight.—We are bivouaced on the
once fine plantation of Gen. Agramonte.—
Received a beautiful boquet from Miss Angel,
a lovely girl.—Weather warm; just like a
Northern July.

"Feb. 2, 1870.—Courier reports the enemy
marching on us, 2,000 strong, and burning
everything in his track.—We are encamped
for the night at St. Tereda, a lovely region of
country. The landscape is beautiful.

"INSPECTOR GENERAL.

"Feb. 23, 1870.—To-day I was appointed
Inspector General, and my name sent to the
Camara (congress) for confirmation as Briga-
dier General.

"6 p. m.—Had a brush with the enemy to-
day. Killed a number, and captured an antique piece of artillery, of the Elizabethan
era. As usual, our boys made quick work of
the foe. The hostile meeting took place
at the Pina plantation. One of the daughters
of Senor Pina killed two Spaniards with a
small revolver, while they were robbing the

mansion. She is as lovely as she is brave and patriotic.

" This afternoon Senor Majora presented me with a fine horse, to replace the one shot under me in to-day's fight."

EXECUTION OF SPANISH SPIES.

Feb. 6, 1870, Gen. RYAN witnessed the execution of three Spanish spies. In noting it in his diary, he says :

"One fell like a hero. He would not kneel, and was permitted to stand while the missiles of death went crashing through his heart. Not a muscle moved, and his face seemed to wear a smile. If in my power I would have pardoned him."

This shows how tender and humane was the heart of the young soldier who subsequently. was barbarously murdered at Santiago de Cuba. RYAN was always ready to bow down to true manliness and courage. Courageous to a fault himself, he admired and respected it even in his enemies.

In another entry in his journal he says :

" Feb. 6, 1870.—To-day issued my first order as Inspector General."

Now, it might be said, commenced his bright Cuban military career.

E

THE CUBAN ARMY.

Now, in reviewing the army, Gen. RYAN found it organized into three grand divisions, with Manuel Quesada General-in-Chief; Gen. Thomas Jordan Chief-of-Staff; Major Beauvilliers Chief-of-Artillery ; "Bembetta" Varona Brigadier-of-Orders ; Adolfo Varona Chief-of-Sanitary Department, and himself (RYAN) Inspector General.

The First Division, or Army of Camaguey, was commanded by Major General Agramonte.

The Second Division, or Army of the Oriente, by General Francisco Aguilera.

And the Third Division, or Army of Las Villas, by Major General Frederic Cavada.

The whole force numbering about 12,000 infantry, cavalry, artillery, etc.

The Division Generals had as subordinates the best officers that could be selected, among whom were Generals Diaz, Castillo, Bosse, Porro, Recio, Coca, Pedro Recio, Bobadillo, Urra, Manuel Agramonte, Marmol, Marcano, Peralta, Acosta, Adolfo Cavada, Hernandez and others, and Colonels Warren, Bailey, Julio Sanguilly, McGill, and Rafael de Varona.

But very few of these gallant leaders lived to hear the sad tidings of the murder of their heroic comrades of the ill-fated Virginius.

Some fell dead, sword in hand, while others were wounded and captured, and suffered untold agony while being inhumanely butchered by the merciless Spaniards.

THE BLOODY WORK.

From the hour of his landing in Cuba until June 17th, 1870, Gen. RYAN was in a series of skirmishes and fierce battles, the most noted of which were the engagements of February 11th, and June 17th and 18th.

February 11th, he encountered the enemy near Puerto Principe, on a reconnoitering expedition. So close were the Insurgents to the city that the enemy's sentinels could be seen walking their posts.

Upon discovering the Insurgents the Spaniards made a grand dash on them, evidently expecting an easy victory. But in this they were greatly disappointed.

The Cubans received them by making a counter charge, Gen. RYAN leading the van, wielding his powerful sabre with terrific and deadly effect.

The Spaniards fought like demons for awhile, but at last broke, and fled in the direction of the city. During the bloody conflict Gen. RYAN and a few of his intrepid men gained the enemy's rear, and when they commenced their disorderly retreat literally cut them to pieces.

In the contest the Spaniards lost 40 killed out of a force of 200. Their principal loss occurred during the retreat.

The Cuban damage consisted of a few dangerous wounds, Gen. RYAN receiving a slight one. A ball struck a button on his jacket and glanced off, ranging across his heart and lodged in his left arm.

The enemy was pursued right up to the walls of the city, where Gen. RYAN planted a flag, and left a small force to guard it while he made a raid along the railroad in the direction of Neuvitas, tore up the track in many places, and cut the telegraph wires.

While thus engaged a small force of Spanish infantry attacked him, but were soon compelled to retreat with considerable loss.

On the 13th of February, General RYAN, Captain Morelle and Lieutenant Cabba, with only 25 men, attacked and put to flight three columns of the enemy in as many consecutive engagements.

Each column of the Spaniards numbered 150 men.

For these brilliant actions the General's command received the highest praises of the commanding Generals.

A BLOODY FIGHT.

The battle of June 17th, 1870, was a very sanguinary one, and as disastrous to the

Spaniards as it was glorious for the invincible Cubans.

The force of General RYAN commenced the action. The Spaniards met the Cubans in splendid style, and for an hour the contest raged fiercely, without either side gaining the advantage. Up to this time nothing but the ring of the gleaming sabre could be heard as they came together with lightning speed, or crushed through some enemy's skull.

But a change soon took place.

A bugle blast rang out from the Cuban ranks to use the pistol.

The left hand quickly grasped the deadly Colt, and the work of blood commenced.

Each of General RYAN's men emptied a saddle at every discharge, and soon, amid the prancing of horses, groans, fire, smoke, crack of pistols and clamor of war, the Spaniards broke into disorder, and precipitately fled, followed by the exultant foe, who cut them down at every jump with the pistol, saber, and the dreadful machette, a very long sword-like knife.

In this terrific fight the Spaniards lost over one hundred in killed, and a number of horses and arms.

The Cubans lost twenty-five killed and a number wounded.

A TERRIBLE BATTLE.

June the 18th, the day following the contest just mentioned, witnessed one of the most terrible dramas ever enacted on the bloody and ghastly theater of war. It occurred in sight of the city of Puerto Principe, and just as the mantle of night was being gently rolled back by the coming dawn.

Gen. RYAN had sent off all his command on a raid, with exception of fifty men. With these he took up a position on the skirt of a small river near Puerto Principe. A bridge ran across this body of water, and formed a portion of the main road to the city. The General anticipated a movement from the Spaniards to seek revenge for the disastrous defeat of the 17th, and accordingly posted himself so that he could watch their actions.

By some means the enemy became aware that the force under General RYAN had been divided.

This was their opportunity. They would rush upon him and sweep him out of existence, and retrieve their lost honors.

Accordingly a force of 450 picked cavalry and infantry were selected for the glorious work.

This plan had no sooner been decided on that it was communicated to General RYAN by one of his negro spies.

After counting the cost, General RYAN determined to ambush, and annihilate the over-confident seekers after revenge. Each of his men had twenty-eight shots, besides their keen-edged swords. With these 1,400 shots, and a judicious use of the trusty sabre, he believed he could utterly destroy those coming to extirpate him.

The enemy would have to cross the bridge to get into the main road, then their route would be flanked for some distance by large trees, and a thick undergrowth of cactus and thorny and gnarled vines.

Just where the road would debouch from this walled defile, Gen. RYAN had stretched a net-work of telegraph wire to trip up the horses. On each side of the road, behind the natural fortification of trees and vines, he posted his men dismounted, save a few at the front and rear of the ambush, to hem in the doomed column. Then he placed two buglers near the bridge, two more near the wire-barricade, and one on each flank.

These were to sound the charge nearly at the same moment; those stationed at the bridge to sound the death knell just as soon as the rear of the Spanish column had entered the path that led to the yawning grave.

At last the fatal hour arrived.

Out from the city poured the heavy dragoons and veteran infantry, four hundred and fifty strong, massed in close column. All was quiet, save the noise of their heavy tramp, tramp, tramp.

It was yet quite dark, but lights gleamed in the city.

At last the little bridge groaned under the heavy weight passing over it.

The "avengers" had entered the fatal passage.

In their rear a strange, shrill bugle blast rings out upon the morning air.

Then it sounds in their front, on their flanks, and all around them.

They halt, and stout hearts shudder.

A loud and continuous report startles the coming day. Horses lose their riders. A wall of fire rises on all sides. The funeral pyre is ablaze. The work of death has commenced. There is no escape. Dead men and horses rapidly fill the defile, and life is narrowing every second.

The work has been done.

Night has disappeared, and the King of Day comes forth to view a terrible scene.

Of those four hundred and fifty souls three hundred and odd are dead or dying.

. And the rest might as well be. None of them will ever cross Carasco bridge alive, save twenty-eight. They all, save one, escaped miraculously ; and he, a mere boy, was spared by Gen. RYAN, and sent to the Governor of Puerto Principe with an account of the awful slaughter.

RETALIATION.

The result of this frightful conflict gave the Cubans an opportunity to drink deep of the sweet cup of revenge, for the inhuman butchery of their mothers, sisters, aged fathers, and brothers and friends made prisoners, and then fiendishly murdered.

One hundred and twenty-two prisoners had been taken by General RYAN.

They were doomed to death.

In one hour after the capture their souls were hurled into eternity, and sent before their God.

It was a fearful sight—four hundred and twenty-one human forms piled up together in gory hideousness.

It was a horrible alternative.

But the Spaniards established the awful precedent, and General RYAN was forced to act in self-defense.

The horrible acts of deviltry committed upon poor, weak and defenseless Cubans had reached monstrous proportions without even an effort at retaliation.

This shocking picture General RYAN determined to hold up to Spanish gaze in their

own brutish gore.   And he shrank not from
the horrible work when opportunity offered.

GEN. RYAN TO THE GOVERNOR.

When this frightful drama of retaliation
was ended, General RYAN wrote the following explanatory letter to the Governor of
Puerto Principe, and sent it by the boy whom
he had spared from the fate that befell his
comrades :

" To THE GOVERNOR OF PUERTO PRINCIPE :
Sir—Your forces and my cavalry have met
on several occasions. In each conflict you
sustained heavy loss. As I expect to meet
them again, I deem it right to apprise
you of the barbarous treatment our women,
children and defenseless old men receive at
the hands of your officers and men. Your
troops, who claim to be honorable soldiers,
murder in the most shocking manner our poor
women and helpless children, mangling their
bodies in the most hideous manner, even to
gouging out their eyes, cutting off their ears
and limbs, and disemboweling them. This
butchery I strongly condemn, while I might
pardon the murder of our soldiers. If you
visited the battle-fields of Cercado, Vista
Hermosa, Magdalena, Manandagua, Delores,
Anton, Horena Cal, La Caridad, Sebastopol,
St. Miguel, and others, you would have seen
how I respected your dead. And now if you

will visit the battle-field of this morning, in full view of your city and forts, you will see how determinedly I can retaliate for the hideous outrages you countenance. There you will find over one hundred of your finest soldiers cut to pieces, stripped of clothing, and scalped. This terrible style of warfare I do not like, but will continue it until your course is changed to that followed by civilized communities. * * This letter will be handed to you by the boy, Manuel Luarez, whose life I spared because of his youth. By him I also send the scalp of one of your Cavalry Majors, and I trust the sight of it will have the effect to bring you to a proper sense of your base conduct. In the engagement of this morning you had 150 Cavalry and 300 Infantry, while I had a mere handful of men. The results of the battle will show you of what material Cuban Patriots are made—men fighting for life, liberty, right and property, and who are determined that their country shall be free from Spanish thraldom.

"In haste, respectfully yours,

"W. A. C. RYAN,

"Gen'l-in-Chief Cuban Cavalry."

This document was perused with a feeling of horror by the Governor, who sent it to Captain General de Rodas immediately.

That functinary was at the theater when it reached him. Thinking it was news of Gen.

Ryan's capture, and probable death, he had the ominous letter read from the stage.

The consternation produced baffles description. The Cuban members of the audience could not restrain a shout of pleasure at the glad tidings, while the loyal element shuddered at the awful picture.

Their unguarded applause was fatal for some of the poor Cubans.

There were present at the time a number of the ferocious Volunteers. When they recovered from the shock produced by the letter, they drew their pistols and commenced indiscriminately firing among the Cuban women and children, killing and wounding quite a number.

VISITING THE GORY FIELD.

The day after the terrible slaughter the Governor, Captain General de Rodas, and other dignitaries visited the battle-field and fully satisfied themselves that General Ryan had done precisely what he said.

He did more. After they left the scene of carnage, he had all the dead humans and horses moved close up to the city walls, and there left to breed pestilence and death, by being exposed to the scorching rays of the June sun.

This induced the authorities to seek an interview with Gen. Ryan for peace purposes.

But it amounted to nothing, in as much as the Spaniards desired the Cubans to end the war by laying down their arms, a proposition scoffed at by the latter.

For this act of retaliation, the Spaniards set a price of $40,000 on Gen. RYAN's head, dead or alive, which accounts for the many attempts made to assassinate the dashing young soldier.

ANOTHER INTERESTING LETTER.

The following letter was not received by his brother, J. G., from General RYAN, until after the two important events of June, just recorded, had transpired. It was written on the 29th of March, 1870, one day after the General's 27th birthday, and dated in camp near Cercada:

"DEAR BROTHER—Since my arrival in Cuba things have been quite lively with us; in fact, a series of skirmishes, and some hard battles. We have to be on the *qui vive* all the time, and are constantly on the move. It might be truly said that our headquarter's, like Pope's, is in the saddle. This is a fearful life. The war presents few civilized features. The Spaniards first flung the *black flag* to the breeze, by indiscriminately murdering defenceless men, women and children, and our soldiers when made prisoners. Their acts are of the most horrible nature, and hid-

eous to look upon. Of course you think a war
of extermination like this would soon end
in disaster to the Cubans. Such a conclusion
is logical, but I assure you that this struggle
will never end while a Cuban rebel breathes.
The infamous cruelties committed upon them
by the barbarous Spaniards have so embit-
tered our people that nothing but their entire
annihilation will restore the island to the
mother country. Just so long as our men
hold out so long will the soil produce subsist-
ence for them. Every species of healthy food
is indigenous to this climate. Fish, fowl,
hogs and cattle about everywhere; and fruits,
vegetables and cereals yield two crops a year,
and require but little cultivation; while the
most nutritious grass springs up all over the
island, affording a rich pasturage for horses
and cows. And the climate being always
summer, we care not if every house is given
to the flames. We have shady trees and cool
recesses in the rugged rocks to shelter our
Spartan women and orphaned children, and
heroic wounded and sick comrades. In fact,
we are so situated that nothing but an army
of half a million of determined men, moved
rapidly, can conquer us. We are all one here
as to color. We have declared the negroes
politically free, and they will die in defence
of those granting the heavenly boon. They
make splendid soldiers, are easily controlled
and desperate in battle. We are one grand

brotherhood, determined to be free or to die in the glorious attempt. And the women, God bless them, are, if such a thing could be possible, more patriotic than the men. They are like sunshine in our gloomy camp. They never murmur, but move about like ministering angels, cheering sad hearts, and casting a halo of brightness wherever they go. And when necessary they can handle the revolver and rifle with deadly accuracy, and many a Spanish trooper has rolled from his saddle when their delicate fingers pressed the fatal trigger. * * We are so impregnably situated that we can slaughter the enemy whenever he approaches. Mountains, rocks, hills, caves, ravines, thick woods, marshy ground, and high grasses afford us protection, and give us incalculable advantage over the foe. Sometimes they leisurely ride into our ambush laughing and singing, and speculating as to the whereabouts of the rebels, not dreaming of danger until the hail of death comes pouring upon them from every side, sounding the dread warning when it too late to save them. It seems like murder. But do *they* deserve *mercy* who *murder* women, children and defenceless old men? "No," I hear you say.**We count twenty-five of our men equal to five hundred of the enemy. ***

"THE CAVALRY CORPS.

"I am now in command of all the Cavalry,

and immediately under me I keep the corps
recently organized. It is a splendid body of
men, and will follow where the most intrepid
dare lead. Its members were carefully selected from the bravest souls of our invincible
army. It would astonish you if I had time
to narrate the wonderful feats of this little
band. When it starts for the enemy it moves
like lightning, and sweeps everything in its
wild march. Its charge is overpowering, ir-
resistible, and fatal to its foes ; the maddened
steeds trample everything in their track, and
the unerring pistol and gleaming sabre complete the awful wreck. * * Quite a number
of prominent officers resigned their positions
in other commands to go into the ranks of
this corps. * * * My Chief of Scouts is
Captain Henry M. Earle Reeves, of Brooklyn, New York, one of best and bravest soldiers that ever drew a sword. At no distant
day he will wear a General's stars. [He is
now, in 1876, a General, and among the most
prominent of the Cuban officers, whom the
Spaniards fear and hate.—ED.] Colonel L.
C. Bailey, of Hoboken, New Jersey, is my
Chief-of-Staff. He is a 'brick.' Colonels
Warren, Clancey, and McGill, are ditto.

"A LIVELY BATTLE.

" Yesterday was my twenty-seventh birthday, and it was celebrated with military

honors. We had a little *surprise* party, and one decidedly unexpected. Colonel Clancy had just set the boys in a roar of laughter by relating the

"MONKEY AND PARROT STORY.

" You may not remember it, so, as it is short I will jog your risibles. A gambler had as pets a parrot and a monkey—both very intelligent. Among the gambler's slang phrases were: 'you bet,' and 'we've had a hell of a time.' These the parrot could speak to perfection. One day during its master's absence, the monkey broke out of its cage and immediately made war on the parrot that had the freedom of the room. In a few minutes the poor bird was as bare of feathers as mother Eve was of clothes when father Adam discovered her in the Garden of Eden. The rascally monkey after gazing upon the forlorn aspect of the unfortunate parrot, and the feathery ruin scattered around the room, ran into its cage and went to sleep. Very soon the gambler and some friends walked in. Upon discovering the carpet strewn with feathers, he was utterly astonished, and exclaimed, 'what in the devil has been going on here?' Here the nude bird stuck its head out from under the bureau, and loudly screamed: 'We've had a hell of a time; you bet.' The way Clancy flourished this was decidedly rich. We had hardly recovered from our laugh when news of the enemy rapidly approaching our camp came suddenly to me. In a moment we were in the saddle, and moving out to interrupt the march of the foe. As Clancy leaped into his saddle he remarked, 'I guess these fellows, when we get through with them, will parrotically exclaim, "we've had a hell of a time, you bet." And it is to be presumed they did. It took me but a few minutes to make ready for the coming storm. Most of my force I placed in ambush on the flanks of the road. A portion of Reeve's Scouts were sent on to meet the enemy, with orders to retreat immediately on coming within sight of him. With my escort and staff I took a position to strike his rear after he had passed through the ordeal of the ambush. In a little while Reeve's rifles were heard. Then the clang of scabbards and heavy tramp of his retreating horse came to our ears. Down past us they flew in close column by fours, pistol ready and sabre gleaming in the noon-day sun. At last the foe entered the vortex of death, and before he became aware of his dread situation sixteen volleys had been poured into his ranks, emptying saddles, and piling up dead horses and riders together. When the opportunity arrived my escort rushed in to play their part in the bloody drama. The Spanish commander now made a masterly move by ordering a retreat, which was executed in splendid style. My escort was so small that it was ridden down in a second by the enemy's heavy dragoons. By this time the ambush flankers advanced with both pistols, and poured a deadly volley into the retreating foe. Reeves had now joined me, and we commenced the pursuit, which lasted for five miles. This action did not last more than thirty-minutes, but in that short space the enemy lost over one hundred men, a number of fine horses, and two hundred pistols and sabres. My loss was twenty-eight seriously wounded. Colonels Clancy and Sanguilly and Capt. Reeves and myself got scratched. One Spanish dragoon literally lifted me out of the saddle. I caught the point of his blade in the hilt of my sword, and saved myself. It was the first time I ever was unhorsed by an enemy. * * * I tell you, Jack, these hireling Spaniards do not like our way of fighting. However, most of the officers are courageous, and die doing their duty.

"GEN. JORDAN LEAVES THE ISLAND.

"I came near forgetting to tell you that General Jordan has been sent to the United States on important business. Congress also detailed me to accompany him on the mission; but Major General Agramonte would not consent to me leaving, unless I insisted on going. Perhaps it may yet be necessary for me to go. * * * I might say that I have now an independent command, and my Cavalry is looked upon as the 'eye of the army.' I must close this, as a courier is about to leave for the coast, and I want it to reach you early. Your last letter, and the Pine Bluff *Press*, reached me O. K. Hope you are well. WHACK."

MORE FIGHTING.

On the 5th of July, 1870, General RYAN scratched a few more lines to his brother, the Colonel. He said:

"Since my letter of the 29th of March we have had the liveliest of times, the action of the 18th ult. being, I must say, the most important. But every day has witnessed a conflict of some kind. On one occasion, while attempting to blow up a train between Puerto Principe, by means of torpedoes, the enemy came near gobbling up myself and small escort. We had to run the gauntlet for life. The enemy had us surrounded. I told the boys we must cut our way out. There were only ten of us. I ordered them into single file at first, as we advanced; then into twos, at a gallop; and gave the order to charge. With our reins between our teeth, and pistol and sabre in hand, we dashed on through a

perfect hell of fire. How we got through is
a mystery to me. But we did it. And it is
hardly to be believed, nevertheless is a fact,
that not a man was seriously hurt. For a
short distance we were pursued by twenty-
five of the enemy. On discovering their
small number, I passed back the word to
'open ranks; halt; about, wheel.' It was
only a minute until they came dashing between our lines. Now it became their turn
to fight for life. A terrific struggle ensued.
Crack, crack, crack, went the pistol, and
clang, thud, clang, thud the terrible sabre,
for some minutes, while the prancing of the
horses and shouts of the combatants added
interest to the bloody scene. It was a struggle on the part of the enemy to get away, and
upon our part to annihilate them. When the
smoke lifted from the scene twenty of the foe
were in full flight, and five of their brave fellows lying dead on the field. We did not follow—for before-mentioned reasons.

"Yesterday was the 'glorious 4th of
July.' I celebrated it by

"HANGING A NOTED SPANISH SPY,

"one Thomas Lopez, a daring fellow. He
died like a hero, without revealing a single
secret. The execution had hardly taken
place when the enemy was reported advanc-
ing. I sent Capt. Harry Reeves to recon-

noitre. Colonels Warren, Clancy and Bailey followed. In a few minutes rapid firing commenced. Now a courier came dashing up with a dispatch that Reeves was in danger. I ordered him to feign a retreat, and directed Clancy and Warren to make flank movements, while I endeavored to gain the enemy's rear. Everything worked well for awhile, but before the foe had got quite into my trap, he ceased his pursuit and commenced a rapid retreat. This movement was executed so unexpectedly and impetuously that I was taken by surprise. I had just debouched into my position when the heavy dragoons came thundering down upon my little escort, and literally trampled it down, in their wild flight. No joke. I, myself, was lifted clean out of the saddle by a stalwart trooper, whose blade ran through my jacket, up to the hilt. His sword getting entangled proved fatal to the gallant fellow, for one of my men ran him through. This was the first time my sword failed to dash aside the enemy's steel. Most certainly the poor trooper must have had a powerful arm.

" RETROSPECTIVE.

"Yesterday, one year ago, myself and 250 splendid fellows were encamped at Gardiner's Island, New York, celebrating the nation's great day. Only for base treachery those men would now be here with me battling for poor Cuba's freedom. * * *

"To-day we had considerable of a frolic, and I feel tired after it. It was at Altamua. Generel Mormol and Captain Maranda did most of the work. The former received several wounds, and the latter had part of his skull knocked off. It did not last twenty-five minutes. Still we lost ten men and fifteen horses. However, we made the enemy suffer heavily. We burned thirty of their dead. We have to cremate the dead, not having time to bury them.

"A CONFERENCE.

"July 9.—Yesterday I had an interview with Generals Agramonte, Boza, Porro, Marmol and Cavada, at Ciego.

"A change of Presidents is in the wind. Some of the leaders are dissatisfied with Cespedes; and this is sympathized with by a majority of the Congress. To-day a commissioner will leave for New York to canvass the matter among our friends there. I will furnish him an escort to the coast. This letter, and one to General Jordan, will be taken by him. It is now 6 p. m., and he will leave at 8. We are again at La Caridad. Very warm here. To-night we will leave for St. Miguel, and expect to attack that city.

"Probably you will never hear from me

again, so adieu. Love to all, when you write.   W. A. C. R."

ATTACK ON ST. MIGUEL.

The evening of July 11, 1870, the Cubans, under Generals Agramonte, Marmol, Boza, Porro and RYAN, attacked the city of Saint Miguel. Major Castillo, of RYAN's Cavalry, a dashing officer, led the advance, and was severely wounded. The fight lasted but a few minutes, the Cubans withdrawing. This was owing to the Artillery not coming up according to orders.

On account of some misunderstanding as to the delay of the Artillery, General RYAN placed in arrest an officer of his old First Cavalry Cuban Liberators, now commanded by the gallant and intrepid Colonel Sanguilly. The latter protested against the arrest of his lieutenant.

This infraction of military discipline on the part of Colonel Sanguilly caused his arrest, also. Becoming very indignant at this, he

SENT GEN. RYAN A CHALLENGE

To fight a duel. The document General RYAN handed to General Agramonte, his superior officer. To have picked up the gauntlet would have laid General RYAN liable to that high military law he so much respected, and without the most implicit obedience to which no efficiency could be expected from the army.

This violation of military law was circumnavigated, however, by General RYAN, who had the Colonel released from arrest.

Shortly afterward the chivalrous but impulsive Sanguilly became aware of his unintentional interference with the just act of his superior officer. An explanation followed, and the cloud passed suddenly away that had let fall its shadow between these true lances of Cuba. And it was well for the cause they did not meet. Both being masters of the pistol and sabre, it is more than likely that one or both would have fallen if Colonel Sanguilly's hasty message had been accepted by General RYAN.

MORE SKIRMISHING.

The following extracts from Gen. RYAN's Diary will show that the Cuban troops were constantly under fire:

"July 12th, 1870.—Had a skirmish this a. m., near St. Thomas. Had negro soldier shot to-day for deserting his post.

"July 13th.—Col. Sanguilly ill. Men in good spirits. Slight skirmish. Gen. Boza arrived this a. m. at 10.

"July 14.—Early this morning had a little brush with the enemy. Their loss ten men:

ours two. 2 p. m.—En route with dispatches for President Cespedes. Met the Misses Merondas. Splendid looking girls. Was received kindly by them. Had Paul Waterford placed under arrest for horse-stealing.

"July 15th.—Col. Lopez Romas scattered the enemy to-day near Saint Thomas. The weather delightful."

WITH PRESIDENT CESPEDES.

July 17, 1870, General RYAN reached tne headquarters of President Cespedes, whom he found in very feeble health. They dined together, and conversed freely about affairs on the Island, and the probable result of the Revolution. After dinner the Secretary of War and several other cabinet officers were announced, who greeted General RYAN heartily. They, like all the true Patriots, dearly loved their gallant American ally.

Soon he was informed by Pres. Cespedes that it had been determined by the Camara (Congress) for him to return to the United States to co-operate with General Jordan in organizing a large expedition, and in placing Cuban matters properly before the American people, through their Congress.

General RYAN was selected for this important mission because of his connection with the United States army during the Rebellion, and on account of his extensive acquaintance

among the most able and influential men of
that nation.

In every respect was Gen. RYAN well qualified to discharge the duties of the important
mission entrusted to him.   His high gentlemanly qualifications, intelligence, courteous
address, and genial and attractive social manners, made him a general favorite, and gave
him the *entree* where influence was to be had.

The announcement that he was to be sent
off on this mission somewhat astonished
our hero, and caused him to offer a protest,
because he had become thoroughly imbued
with the Insurgent cause on the Island, notwithstanding the life of war was one fraught
with the most trying hardships, and had entered the bloody field with the determination
not to leave it until the dread drama was
over, or he had fallen on the crimsoned altar
of poor Cuba's freedom.

But, like a true soldier, he at last bowed
to the will of his superiors, and listened to
the instructions given him for his guidance
on his new mission.

RETURN TO NEW YORK.

On taking leave of President Cespedes and
his Cabinet, General RYAN immediately proceeded to the headquarters of Gen. Frederic
Cavada, the recently appointed Commander-
in-Chief of the Army, and his warm personal

friend. Their meeting was of the usual cordial character. They freely discussed all matters bearing upon the mission, and determined upon the most expeditious course to be followed to successfully carry out the project.

As General Cavada was personally and favorably known to President Grant, having served faithfully and honorably under him during the late Great Rebellion in the United States, and General B. F. Butler, and other distinguished gentlemen, he addressed each autograph letters imploring them to lend an ear to the statements of poor Cuba's commissioner. This done, and other necessary preparations made for the trip, a convocation of the prominent officers in the secret, and some personal friends of minor importance, was held, and a good social time had.

This convivial parting over, the dashing young cavalier started for the coast on his important undertaking.

Before leaving he had the gallant Captain W. S. Ashley, late of North Mississippi, appointed Colonel of Cavalry. This gentleman, as appears from General RYAN's Diary, has relatives in Aberdeen, Miss. Probably now, in 1876, the poor fellow's bones, like those of his martyr commander, are bleaching beneath the rays of suffering Cuba's sun.

General RYAN received permission for his Chief-of-Staff, Col. L. C. Bailey, to accompany him, and together they safely reached the coast, under escort of Colonel Ashley.

THE PERILOUS TRIP.

It would be most injudicious to relate by what means General RYAN succeeded in making his exit from the Island, because such relation would be furnishing information to the enemies of Cuba. It is enough to say that he accomplished it at the imminent risk of his life from the Spaniards first, the wild beasts of the jungle second, and the turbulent waters of the Gulf of Mexico third.

To the uninitiated it would seem a great feat, and a matter of supreme wonder how it was accomplished. The author was in the same perplexity as the reader once. To him such a thing seemed without the region of possibilities, surrounded as the Island was, and is, by Spanish war vessels of almost every class, constantly moving about patrolling the coast. It would seem as though a duck could scarcely escape detection.

ARRIVAL IN NASSAU.

August 6, 1870, Gen. RYAN and Colonel Bailey, after a hazardous journey, and many hairbreadth escapes from being picked up by Spanish cruisers, found themselves safely and comfortably ensconced at the American hotel in Nassau, N. P., surrounded by a number of delighted and astonished friends, who greeted them warmly.

On the 9th of August, after a delightful stay, they left for Key West, where they arrived on the 13th, at 10 a. m. By 12 m. their hotel was crowded with visitors, and in the evening they were the recipients of a

GRAND BANQUET,

given by the citizens of the place and foreign dignitaries and visitors ; a number of United States Army and Navy officials being, also, present.

On the 15th of August a Cuban mass-meeting was held, and very largely attended. Gen. RYAN delivered a short speech, full of interesting Cuban war statistics, which was enthusiastically received. The Spanish consul was present, and could not disguise his chagrin at the enthusiasm in favor of the Cubans.

On the 17th of August General RYAN and Colonel Bailey, accompanied by a large concourse of admirers, stepped on board the steamship Ariadne and sailed for New York.

Before leaving Key West Gen. RYAN telegraphed his brother at Pine Bluff, Ark., to meet him immediately in New York, at Lelands' Metropolitan hotel. Col. J. G., on receipt of the dispatch, quietly closed his law books, laid aside his editorial pen, bid adieu to a few friends, and "skimmed out," as he said, for the Empire city, where both arrived nearly simultaneously.

ARRIVAL IN NEW YORK.

It is hardly necessary to state that General RYAN received a right royal welcome on his return to New York, but for the information of those who will peruse these pages when the author has passed from this earthly sphere, he will say that the reception accorded his gallant young hero was such as would challenge the admiration of a jealous potentate. For several days after his arrival at the Metropolitan hotel his rooms were perfectly packed with bewitching woman and gallant men—some old friends, and others stranger admirers—but all anxious to see the dashing young Cuban Patriot.

In the hotel lobbies, on the streets or the avenues, in the public parks, or on the fashionable walks or drives, it was all the same, he was the center of attraction as his tall, fine form, broad-brimmed sombrero and long, curling hair came into view.

And among those who paid the deepest homage to the daring and successful soldier were those of the Cuban element who had suffered most at the hands of their implacable enemies, the Spaniards. They hailed him at every turn to pour out their heartfelt thanks for his noble efforts in their behalf, and aged men and women, and lovely girls wept tears of joy as their young bronzed-faced defender poured into their ears words of hope—that the glorious day was not far distant when the sun would no longer set on the thraldom of their beloved country.

The brilliant reception given to the distinguished General Thomas Jordan paled into common-place when compared to that tendered to Gen. RYAN by his Cuban friends, and the great mass of the people sympathizing with their struggle for independence. It was an outpouring of gratitude bubbling up from the deepest depths of the Cuban heart, and rippling away into sweeping waves of impassioned feeling. No illustrious man ever received a grander acknowledgment of a brave people's love.

And our dashing hero deserved it all. Twenty-seven years had but just crowned his head with manhood. Still he stood out before the world wreathed with a wealth of glory and fame seldom falling to the lot of the most favored of God's creatures.

And this homage was not from the Cubans alone. From the representatives of most, if not all, of the great powers of the globe adulation was poured upon him in a constant and brilliant stream. Ministers, ambassadors, consuls, army and navy officials, and private citizens of wealth and distinction, were ever ready and anxious to greet the daring young "filibuster." Even the haughty Spaniard could not but admire the chivalrous Phil. Sheridan or "Jeb." Steuart of Cuban Cavalry fame. And among the lovely Spanish ladies who graced Washington society many smiled graciously upon him. One especially, whom he first met at Key West. She was a bewitching creature. A sweet letter of hers to him, found among his papers, indicated the strongest Platonic affection. She evidently was a person of rare attractions, else she never would have attracted the following comments, copied from one of his Journals:

THE SPANISH BEAUTY.

" * * * Assuredly she is one of the most bewitching creatures I have ever met. Her face is surpassingly lovely, her form and carriage queenly, her movements faultless grace, her mouth like split cherries; her eyes black as night, dreamy in repose, but flashing like diamonds when under excitement. Her voice is beyond my powers of description—full, fresh, sweet and melodious, and when in song is perfectly entrancing. How she implored me to desert the 'vile Cubans,' as she styled my adopted people. She depicted my probable future in the most hideous colors; and said that the garrote was

F

waiting to drink my blood, as it had that of the gray-haired martyr, General Goicouria. She is very loyal to her country. How strange it is! Here is this angelic creature, at whose feet a monarch would feel proud to kneel in reverence, counseling me for what she considers my good. Still I am not particularly affected by her charms. My heart is yet my country's. Who knows! probably she will live to see her prediction realized as to my death. This I told her, and I never will forget the look of agony that flashed across her lovely face. Well, no matter. Time will tell. * * "

Poor RYAN! it is scarcely probable he then thought that in three short years his lifeless body would be trampled into the gutter by the iron hoofs of Spanish dragoons; brutally butchered in cold blood, without the semblance of a fair and impartial trial. But when he fell beneath the murderous fire of Spanish hirelings, at the nod of *"Butcher"* *Burriel*, he pictured, in startling colors, to the whole world how a Cuban Patriot could die; and left behind a record that those ambitious for honor and fame will always love to emulate.

INTERVIEWED.

As a natural consequence, Gen. RYAN had scarcely changed his battle-tattered garb for

that of the promenade ere the genial commissioners of the leading press called and gave
him a hearty welcome. He was always a
favorite with the newspaper men, and no
man could more highly appreciate them as
a class, nor knew the importance of their
friendship in a cause such as he had cast his
fortunes. He often was heard to say that if
the newspaper men, Reporters to begin with,
of New York, Philadelphia, Brooklyn, New
Orleans, Chicago, Charleston, etc., could
have been manipulated by Spanish gold the
death knell of Cuban independence would
have been sounded in 1869—so far as the
people of the United States were concerned.

The lively *Sun* man was ahead of his en-
terprising contemporaries in this instance,
and "scooped" in the General before he
left the steamship. The next morning that
journal contained a very interesting two-
column "interview," which gave a very
good insight into the affairs on the Island.
As the reader is already aware of most of the
information gleaned by the reporter, only
the new facts will be introduced, as follows:

"Yes," said the General, as he and the
knight of the quill sipped their iced wine in
the luxurious cabin of the vessel, as she lazily
steamed up the river, "yes, sir, our cause is
flourishing rapidly. We now have an army
of about 12,000 as well drilled and discip-

lined and effective troops—infantry, cavalry and artillery—as ever faced an enemy. We hold half of the Island, that part east of Puerto Principe. At times we have raided to within a few miles of Havana. In the Cam aguey District, that nearest the main body of the the enemy, where I have operated, the hardest fighting has been done. Besides countless skirmishes, I have been in

"THIRTY-THREE BATTLES

"of considerable magnitude with my Cavalry, and never lost but one of them, and that was where I attacked 1,500 with a force of scarcely 100. Still we escaped with little or no loss. Of course we have the advantage of position. I count one of our men equal to 25 of the enemy. For six months I never slept under a roof, the country is houseless. What the enemy left General Cavada ordered destroyed, that the foe would have no shelter. No, the ladies do not complain at this hardship, they are truly Spartan in their devotion to the cause. Soon not a house will be standing in the Cinco Villas District. An edict has gone forth to raze every one to the ground. So, in the future, the women and children must find shelter behind rocks and in caves.

"IT IS A FEARFUL WAR,

"and made truly horrible by the *black flag*

having been swung to the breeze by both
sides. The Spaniards inaugurated it by the
most ferocious acts of cruelty and hellish bar-
barity, both upon soldiers and defenceless
women and children, ever chronicled. But
we make it fearfully hot for them in return.
* * A few weeks ago the Spaniards brutally murdered our General Marmol's entire
family, consisting of fifteen members, all women and children. The fate of his two beautiful daughters was frightful. The were

" SUBJECTED TO THE BASE LUST

of the demon soldiers, and afterwards put to
death. Is it possible, sir, that God will give
victory to a flag that countenances such monstrous atrocities! Surely not. * * The
Cubans suffer terribly. * * Yes, sir, the

" LIBERATED NEGROES

"fight splendidly. * * No man was more
esteemed than Gen. Jordan. * * * Our
old Federal comrade, General Cavada, and
General Agramonte, are the rising lights of
the Revolution. * * * New York's gallant son, Col. Harry Reeves, if he lives, will
make his power felt. My Chief-of-Staff, Col.
L. C. Bailey, of Hoboken, whom you just
met, has made an enviable record. * * *
My mission to this country is for the purpose
of making an effort to induce the government

to recognize Cuba's independence, and if not that, then her belligerency, that we may enjoy the same privileges in her military warehouses that are accorded to Spain. I have

"STRONG LETTERS

"to President Grant, Gen. Ben. F. Butler, Senator Henry Wilson, and many other prominent Americans, besides to the representatives of the governments of England France and Germany, urging this matter. I hope to accomplish much. * * President Cespedes is in such poor health that he may soon retire from his office. * * * * Since Gen. Jordan left the Island the disposition of affairs have necessarily been materially altered. The District of Santiago de Cuba is commanded by Major Gen. Marmol; Holquin by Major Gen. Julio Peralta; Tunis by Major Gen. Vincente Garcia; Camaguey by Major Generals Agramonte and Manuel Roja; Santa Esperitu by Major Gen. Garcia; Remedios by Major Gen. Hernandez; Trinidad by Major Gen. Frederic Cavada; Bayamo by Major Gen. Modesto Diaz. All fine soldiers. * * "

SWORD AND FLAG PRESENTATION.

A few days after General RYAN's return to New York his enthusiastic Cuban friends, among whom were a number of ladies, gath-

ered at Delmonico's and presented him with
a magnificent sword and elegant silk flag,
as a token of their high appreciation of his
services for the cause of their beloved
country. Madame Villaverde, one of Cuba's
most patriotic daughters, delivered the exquisite presentation address. "No more patriotic lady ever unfurled a banner," says
Gen. RYAN's Diary.

MORE TROUBLE.

Aug. 26, 1870, had arrived. That night
the late Colonel Jim Fisk—so brutally murdered by Ed. Stokes, now, in 1876, serving a
short term in Sing Sing prison for his cowardly act—and his celebrated Ninth regiment
New York State Guards, were to give one of
their grand balls at the magnificent Contin-
ental hotel, Long Branch. General RYAN
was complimented with invitations for himself, Col. L. C. Bailey, Dr. H. T. Peck, and
his brother, Col. J. G. At 4 p. m. the quartette stepped into a carriage at the Metropolitan hotel and drove down to the steamer
Plymouth Rock.

Just as the party were about leaving the
carriage U. S. Deputy Marshal Allen stepped
up and informed the General that he was

HIS PRISONER,

and requested him to accompany him to the

U. S. Commissioner's office on Chambers street. At the General's invitation Marshal Allen took a seat in the carriage, and they were all driven to the court room.

Upon inquiry, the General learned that his arrest was upon a warrant setting forth that the June previous, as will be remembered, he had caused the *abduction* of U. S. Marshal Downey, thereby obstructing the law. It was generally believed that that matter had been long since satisfactorily settled. Nevertheless, it was a patent fact that trouble was ahead for the General, with every indication that *Spanish gold* was working evil for him.

After considerable circumlocution the General was arraigned before U. S. Commissioner Shields, who plead want of jurisdiction in the case. Finally, District Attorney Purdy signified his willingness to shoulder the responsibility, and concluded to set the General at liberty on a

BOND OF $25,000.

This announcement perfectly astonished the large concourse present. The enormous bond was considered without a precedent, and strongly savoring of persecution.

While these preliminaries were going on the General's brother left the court-room and was soon whirling off in a carriage for the

Sun office. On arriving there he found the
editor, Gen. Charles A. Dana, absent. But
Colonel Cummins was present. To him the
situation was made known. Quietly he put
aside his editorial proofs and stepped into the
carriage. Then they drove for Judge Stuart
and Barretson Redfield, another attorney of
General RYAN. In a few minutes these gentlemen entered the presence of Attorney
Purdy, shook the General's hand, smiled upon the crowd, and—made the excessive bond,
much to the noticeable annoyance of a few
Spanish agents who made the dark ground
to the animated picture.

Thus was frustrated a Spanish plot to prevent General RYAN from reaching Long
Branch that night, where he expected to meet
quite a number of prominent gentlemen on
Cuban business. That there was an unseen
and malignant influence at work was very
evident, because the warrant had been issued
several days, during which time Gen. RYAN
was to be found at any hour at his hotel.

After the bond was signed, the General
and his friends, including a number of newspaper men, adjourned to Delmonico's restaurant and drank Cuba's health in refreshing
wine.

Then the General and his party resumed
their journey, and arrived at the Branch just
as the doors of the grand *salon* were being

thrown open, and the joys of the evening commencing. As they drove up to the broad piazza the splendid band was playing one of Prince Erie's favorite airs, "Tassels on her boots," but when Colonel Fisk discovered Gen. RYAN the music was suddenly changed to "The conquering hero comes," and when it became known that he was present the vast assemblage gave a loud cheer for Cuba, while countless friends gathered around to shake his hand. None was more gracious than the gallant Col. Fisk, radiant in gorgeous diamonds and elegant uniform. He took the General's arm and chaperoned him through the dense mass of beauty, chivalry, rich laces and exquisitely wrought, attractive and costly apparel, and at last left him in beauty's circle, whirling in the mazes of the entrancing and soul-enthraling dance.

The ball was a magnificent affair.

In speaking of it, a correspondent alluded to Gen. RYAN in this way:

"The dashing General RYAN was among the most prominent present. He is a magnificent looking fellow; soldierly in every move, and as graceful as handsome. He is tall, erect, and broads-houldered; wears his dark-brown hair long, curling, and thrown carelessly back from a broad and massive forehead; his dark-blue eyes fairly laugh, and his delicately chiselled mouth curls with

a sncy air very attractive. It may justly be
said that he was the focus of all the bright
eyes of the dance. His recent war hardships
leave no trace of pain upon his youthful but
bronzed face. His brother, a rather independent, haughty, Southernized person, was
with the General. It is said their love for
each other is as rock-rooted as was that of
the ' Corsican brothers.'   *   *   *.''

THE MISSION.

Just so soon as General RYAN rested from
the fatigue of his trip from Cuba he entered
with vigor upon the business entrusted to his
care. In this he was ably seconded by Gen.
McMahon, President of the American Cuban
League, Gen. Thomas Jordan, Madame Villaverde, Hon. Geo. Francis Train, the since
murdered Hon. Mansfield Walworth, Dr. H.
T. Helmbold, Col. Jim Fisk, and a number
of others sympathizing with the cause. He
presented his letters to President Grant, Gen.
Butler, and others, and was well received
by all. He also waited on his much valued
friend, the late Vice President Henry Wilson,
and Congressmen Carpenter, Voorhees, Lo-
gan, Banks, Cox, Butler, Morton, Blaine,
Cavanaugh, Fenton, Nye of Nevada, and
many more prominent leaders, and implored
their aid in behalf of his suffering people.

How well he discharged his important

office Messrs. Banks, Cavanaugh and Voorhees could well testify if so disposed to
speak, and to refer to those "*papers.*"

He left nothing undone to gain for poor
Cuba a hearing before the great judgment
bar of the American people. His appeals
for sympathy being strongly indorsed by the
New York *Sun, Herald* and *Tribune,* and
most of the leading journals of the country.

FRANCO-IRISH SYMPATHY MEETING.

The evening of Sept. 12, 1870, was an interesting occasion in Cooper Institute, New
York. That large hall was perfectly packed
with men and women, assembled to express
sympathy for the French people in their war
with Germany. The audience was principally composed of Irish and French, with a
sprinkling of Americans and Cubans. The
rostrum was beautifully festooned with the
American, French, Irish and Cuban flags.
Eminent orators were present, and General
RYAN was among the invited guests. He appeared on behalf of struggling Cuba, and
when called upon delivered a speech that elec-
trified the audience, and drew forth prolonged shouts that "Cuba must be free."

In this effective manner he was influencing
those who represented the people in the national legislature, that they might soon decide
to recognize Cuba as a sister republic.

Again he unfurled the red white and blue lone star flag where he could touch the nation's heart, and hear its patriotic throbs. It was on the occasion of the

FARRAGUT FUNERAL,

Sept. 30, 1870, a day occupying at least one indelible page in the nation's history, for it witnessed the consignment to their last resting place of the mortal remains of the immortal Admiral Farragut, the Nelson of the American navy, and a man without a peer as a patriot, soldier, and noble gentleman. Among the sincere mourners was Gen. RYAN. Notwithstanding the drenching rain, frightful lightning and crashing thunder of the fearfully gloomy day, he was out assisting at the sacred ceremonies, with the Cuban flag draped in black. Dr. H. T. Helmbold generously tendered his magnificent six-in-hand for him and party, consisting of Generals Safford and Holmes, and Colonels L. C. Bailey and J. G. Ryan. Commenting on the procession the New York *Sun* said:

" The only turnout in the procession whose occupants dared face the pitiless storm was the carriage containing the Cuban representatives. The Cuban flag waved gracefully over the heads of its supporters, and as it passed the several regiments of New York troops they *saluted it* by presenting arms, a mark of respect of which our government should take notice."

SECOND ANNIVERSARY OF CUBAN INDEPENDENCE.

October 10, 1870, the Cubans in New York celebrated the second anniversary ot the unfurling of the flag of independence at Yara, by President Cespedes, and others. It was held in Cooper Institute, and was a grand occasion. Senor Matre presided, and speeches were made by Generals Jordan, McMahon and RYAN, and Senors Don Jose Mester, Cuban Commissioner to the United States; Padre Jose Palma, a priest ot the Spanish Episcopal church; Jose Maria Cespedes, Dr. F. Ruz, Jose de Arma, Col. Eurique Agramonte, and M. Petil, a French gentleman. Amid the booming of artillery, martial music, fluttering of flags, and shouts of the excited multitude, the ceremonies commenced. Reports said that for a long time Gen. RYAN remained hid from view, behind festoons of flags, enjoying the scene with Miss Fannie A. Lockrow, and other ladies. But soon his name rang out high above all other sounds; and the "fighting General," as he was styled, had to step forward and deliver an address, which he did in a masterly style, and called forth such thunders of applause as to convince the most sceptical that he had a bright place in the pure Cuban heart.

THE HORNET EXPEDITION.

While the uninitiated imagined that Gen. RYAN was devoting the waning summer and autumn to dashing around among society belles, he was in reality exercising his active brain devising plans for another expedition, which was afterward so nationally known as that of the famous steamer Hornet, which was just then released from United States custody. When she was secretly chartered she was ordered to Aspinwall to await the arrival of the steamer Ocean Queen, on which General RYAN was to sail.

When the time arrived to leave, General RYAN designedly let the Spanish spies hear that he was going off on the steamer Morro Castle. Valise in hand he stepped into a carriage in front of the Metropolitan hotel, and was leisurely driven to the vessel. Jauntingly he walked up the gang plank, bid the "porter" adieu, and entered the cabin.

This *porter* was the *driver* who, it will be remembered, figured in the Marshal Downey escapade in June 1869. She was still faithful to her trust.

In a few minutes after going on the steamer Gen. RYAN left it, disguised as a laborer, and quietly walked off in the direction of Broadway, where he rejoined the "porter." Two days later he sailed for Aspinwall on the Ocean Queen.

If Gen. RYAN had left on the Morro Castle the Spanish authorities would have had him arrested at Charleston, S. C.

AT ASPINWALL.

Dec. 12, 1870, the Ocean Queen arrived at Aspinwall, with Gen. RYAN on board.

From notes in his Diary, it is evident the General was disappointed in not finding the number of men and munitions of war that he expected. And besides this, the steamer Hornet was behind time.

While awaiting the Hornet's coming, to take the men and munitions to Cuba, General RYAN took a trip across the Isthmus to Panama. While there his presence created con siderable excitement, the natives thinking he was about to inaugurate a revolution, a not uncommon, but very frequent occurrence in that region.

On his return to Aspinwall, Christmas day, the General had his men marshalled before his hotel, Betancourt, the American and Cuban flags thrown to the breeze, and a volley of rejoicing fired. This amusement renewed the rumors set afloat at Panama, and soon a large body of armed natives gathered, and commenced an attack upon the revellers. Quite a number of shots were fired before the disturbance was quelled, which was only brought about through the agency of Mr.

Crampton, the British consul. Fortunately no one was seriously injured.

While in Aspinwall General RYAN was a special guest at a magnificent Masonic levee, and was in other respects handsomely treated by the residents of the city.

THE HORNET'S ARRIVAL AND DEPARTURE.

Dec. 29, 1870, the "lightning" Hornet arrived at Aspinwall, the expedition was placed on board, and on the 31st she departed for the Island of Cuba.

On the 5th of January, 1871, the vessel's boiler's needing repairs, she put into Port Triburon, or Shark Bay, on the Haytian coast, 160 miles from Port au Prince.

Here an amusing incident occurred. While the repairs were going on General RYAN, the Captain of the vessel, and the General's aids, took a stroll into the little, dilapidated town at the head of the bay. As they left the mud pier they were halted by a dusky soldier in a garb inferior to and umbrella struck by lightning. The antique oracle propounded a thousand and one questions, at the same time looking at the new-comers suspiciously. The piece of consequence was no less a person than the commandant of the place. This information was gleaned by Gen. RYAN saying, in answer to the uncouth fellow's impudent questions :

" Well, now, who in h—l are you?"

"I iz de guvment," was the reply.

This astounding information was accompanied with the assertion that the party must ogo with him to the headquarters of the commanding General, which they did. That functionary, when he learned the cause of their presence on his territory, treated them courteously. However, while they were sipping a glass of Madeira with him some of the men on the vessel discharged a howitzer. This created the greatest consternation, and for a time

JEOPARDIZED THEIR LIVES,

for the natives rapidly assembled, thinking the place was being bombarded, and fiercely threatened their deaths, unless the attack was immediately stopped. At last things were quieted, a friendly parting took place, and the amused sight-seekers returned to the vessel, which soon steamed for Cuba.

NEARLY CAPTURED.

January 7, 1871, the Hornet sighted Cuba. She was under a full head of steam and all sail set at the time, and making for her intended port like lightning. when boom, boom, boom, thundered forth from a Spanish vessel hid from view behind a rocky point, and the shot came whistling through her rigging, creating considerable arm.

Quick as a flash the Captain ordered the vessel's course changed. She spun around like a top, and darted away like the wind, while the heavy iron from the enemy's cannon plowed the waters in her wake.

It was a narrow escape.

THE LANDING.

At 11 o'clock that same night anchor was cast near Puenta Brava, and the situation on shore reconnoitered. Everything appearing safe, a landing of the expedition was effected, and by daylight of January 8, 1871, it was on its way to the Insurgent headquarters.

PORT AU PRINCE, HAYTI.

She having fulfilled her mission, Gen. RYAN ordered the Hornet into safe quarters, and on the 10th of January she steamed into Port au Prince, and anchored near the United States war vessel Severn.

While Gen. RYAN was with the Hornet at Port au Prince the Spanish minister endeavored to induce Admiral Lee to seize her. But that gallant officer refused to do so, unless ordered by United States Consul Bassett. And the latter was firm in his position that he had no such authority to give.

When this failed, the Spaniards of the war vessel Isabella Catolica made a plot to seize the Hornet, but it died in its infancy, because of the presence of, the Severn.

BACK TO NEW YORK.

Gen. RYAN having accomplished his mission returned to New York, where he safely arrived on the 6th of February, 1871. On reaching the great metropolis he was waited on by a *Sun* reporter, to whom he emphatically denied the report of the Spaniards that he, or any friends of Cuba, had intended seizing the steamer Ocean Queen and converting her into a Cuban privateer. But the Spaniards still contended that such was the case.

PROGRESS OF THE CUBAN WAR.

Ever since General RYAN left the Island up to the landing of the Hornet expedition the struggle was continued to be prosecuted in the most vigorous manner, each day's bloody work strengthening the cause of the suffering Insurgents. Quite a number of changes had taken place. On the Spanish side Captain General DeRodas had been laid on the shelf and Count Valmaseda placed in his stead. This occurred Dec. 10, 1870. On the Insurgent side death, sickness and resignations caused many alterations. Gen. Diaz was in command of the East, with Generals Gomez,

Inclan and Figuerdo commanding Divisions. Gen. Garcia Chief of Camaguey, with Generals Agramonte and Vega commanding Divisions. Gen. Casanova commanding the department of Las Villas, with Generals Juan Villegas, Villamil, Ruloff and Hernandez Division commanders. The forces, all told, under these officers numbered about 11,000 tried and true warriors, always ready for the terrible strife.

THE ILLUSTRIOUS DEAD.

Up to February, 1871, among the illustrious dead who fell for Cuba's sake were the following. Some died in the heat of battle, others were made prisoners and butchered, while many were taken to Havana or Santiago de Cuba and executed by the *garrote*, an instrument of torture and death resembling a barber's chair. Into this the victim is placed, his arms and legs bound fast, an iron band placed around his neck, to which a screw is affixed. This is gradually turned with a crank, and his life squeezed out. This was the fate of the first one on the roll of honor, as annexed. All were strong friends of Gen. RYAN, and it was with feelings of sadness he used to refer to the *missing roll*. Here follows the list:

General Goicuria, General Marmol, Leon Medina, Gen. F. Aguero, Colonel Angarica,

Antonio Jiminez, H. Castillo, Colonels Portuondo, Medal, Garcia, Mercedes Varona, V. Goicuria, O. Cespedes, G. Guitteras, Col. Figuerdo, Luis Arudondo, Luis Agnera, A. Castillo, Maria Guerra, General Arango, and Luis Aysteran.

On one occasion, at a commemoration service, Gen. RYAN made an address, in which he referred to the fallen Patriots as follows:

" My friends, the holy duty we perform is no more than what is due the memory of those noble souls who, to-day, look down upon us from their grand celestial home among the angels. No honor we can confer upon their memory will add to their glorious records. As patriots they lived and as martyrs they died, and the dews of Heaven never fell softly upon more hallowed graves. And it is our sacred duty to live and die as they have done, that future gatherings like these may strew flowers upon our last resting places, as we do upon theirs, and to rejoice in tears of sorrow and pride; in sorrow, because we are gone forever; and in pride, because we died as only martyrs die who draw the sword for liberty."

Poor RYAN! probably then a chill of the future stole softly over his soul. But if there did, it came unnoticed by the great heart whose throbbing it would still.

MONTANER, THE OUTLAW.

Among the most noted, infamous and cruel of the Spanish cut-throats was the human fiend Montaner, commander of a band of guerillas. No deed was too dastardly for him to perpetrate, and no obstacle too formidable for him to attempt to surmount. He was as desperate and courageous as he was inhuman and devilish. His deeds were horrible, and he delighted in the foulest murders.

This wretch had a great desire to meet Generals RYAN and the gallant "Bembetta" Varona in action, a feeling that was heartily reciprocated by them. General RYAN never met him, but Varona did on two occasions. In the first place Montaner came near capturing him while an invalid from wounds, and sojourning with his friend Cristobal Mendoza, residing near Puerto Principe. Fortunately, however, he received news of the raid just in time to escape. But his friend Mendoza was wounded, captured, taken to Puerto Principe, and murdered November 28, 1870.

This cowardly act determined Gen. Varona to seek Montaner and wipe him out of existence. In a few adys Col. Harry Reeves succeeded in drawing the outlaws into a trap, and

MONTANER WAS KILLED.

The contest was short, but fierce. The

outlaw chief died hard, and not until his gleaming sabre had described a circle of death around him. While he was closely pressing Varona, the latter's orderly, a brave and faithful negro, put a pistol to his head and blew out his brains. Then his band precipitately fled. Gen. Varona received the guerilla's sword, and sent it to New York to General RYAN as a trophy.

When Montaner fell, one of the most devilish brutes that ever disgraced humanity passed out of existence.

APPEAL TO THE UNITED STATES FOR RECOGNITION.

Affairs now looking so promising for the Cubans, it was considered politic to bring the matter of their recognition before the United States Congress. The effort was made, but it signally failed, notwithstanding the herculean efforts of the late Vice President Wilson, and Hons. Dan Voorhees, S. S. Cox, N. P. Banks, and delegate Cavanaugh of Montana, in behalf of the move. This indifferent action of Congress greatly surprised the great body of the American people who were anxious to see Cuba freed from Spanish thraldom.

"OUR SOCIETY."

When the recognition scheme failed before Congress, General RYAN suddenly appeared before the public as the publisher and head of a first-class journal called *Our Society*, published in New York, and devoted specially to the movements of *bon ton* society. This unexpected change from the sword of war to the pen of peace was the cause of considererable astonishment and comment on the part of the general public. But their curiosity was soon satisfied when Spanish spies ferreted out the fact that the paper was purchased for the purpose of keeping the Cuban cause properly before the wealthy and influential of the nation.

While conducting this paper, which was considered one of the most elegantly gotten up in the world, General RYAN became involved in a suit at law with O. D. Taylor, a Wall street banker. During the investigation of the case, which was decided in favor of General RYAN, Taylor's attorney, Col. Robt. N. Waite, reflected unwarrantably upon the General, who immediately resented the insult by attempting to slap his face. This act induced the doughty Colonel

TO CHALLENGE GEN. RYAN

to fight a duel. This was accepted, and Gen. RYAN sent his friend, Capt. John W. Fenton, to the Colonel's friend, Dr. Wm. J. Pursell, to arrange for the meeting, having directed him to name Colt's navy, and to advance after first the fire. However, no meeting took place. Colonel Waite would not fight, nor apologize. So General RYAN published him in the papers as a "coward and paltroon." This occurred in September 1871.

In December, 1874, the author had the pleasure of meeting Capt. Fenton in Washington, D. C. In referring to this affair he said :

"Sir, Gen. RYAN was the embodiment of honor. He never gave, nor would he tamely brook an insult. His ideas of satisfaction between gentlemen partook of the old school of chivalry, and he observed its laws jealously. I knew him ever since he was a mere boy in the 132nd New York volunteers, fighting for the Union. And from that time until he fell a victim to Spanish tyranny I never knew him to do an ungentlemanly act. He was an extraordinary young man, and if he had lived there is no telling what glories would have encircled his brow. * *."

The middle of 1872 General RYAN withdrew from *Our Society*, it having accomplished its purpose.

DEATH OF GENERAL CAVADA.

Before retiring from the tripod it was Gen. RYAN's painful office to record the murder of his gallant comrade General Frederic Cavada, one of the bravest souls that ever drew a sword for liberty. He fell wounded at the head of his men, was captured, and shot on the 1st of July, 1871, notwithstanding the protests of the prominent officials of the United States, President Grant included. A fact that proved conclusively at what a discount the Spaniards rated the government of uncle Sam. The dashing Cavada's dying words were:

"My only regret is that I have not just such a life to offer up each and every day until the freedom of my persecuted country is established. I have not asked for pardon, and would not accept it at Cuba's dishonor. Cuba must be free."

Like Marshal Ney, he died with his face to the foe, and a smile on his bronzed and battle-scarred face. Cavada and RYAN, Varona, Agramonte, Martinez, Arango, Marmol, Goicuria and Aguera, were strong friends, and they all fell like heroes.

ANOTHER EFFORT FOR RECOGNITION.

In February, 1872, General RYAN made another effort to induce the United States to even accord to Cuba belligerent rights. A carefully prepared statement of facts upon which the appeal was based was gotten up by Cuban Commissioners Francisco V. Aguilera and Ramon Cespedes, and laid upon the desk of every Congressman. Congressmen

Voorhees of Indiana, Myers of Pennsylvania, Nye of Nevada, Cox of New York, Banks of Massachusetts, and others, again raised their patriotic voices and poured forth their eloquence in behalf of down-trodden Cuba. But, alas! this effort, too, failed, and those battling for liberty were left to struggle on without a hope of succor from a government, the people of which fully sympathized with their cause.

In the full belief that this appeal to Congress would prove successful the prominent Cubans organized themselves into a huge bank, and had issued millions of dollars in bonds, for the redemption of which private estates were pledged.

While the question of recognition was being discussed in Congress, one Capt. Francis L. Norton gained a little cheap notoriety by attacking the position of General Banks through the New York *Express*. Perhaps Spanish gold stimulated his pen.

The speeches of Messrs. Voorhees and Banks on this occassion were ponderous, logical and convincing, and did great honor to their heads and hearts, as well as credit to the great body of liberty-loving Americans, and elevated them to enviable places in the breasts of every freeman throughout this glorious land.

Mr. Voorhees supported his position by

stating that the Spaniards had on seven occasions torn down and trampled upon the stars
and stripes, and that at least four brilliant
Americans had been fiendishly tortured to
death at their hands on the 10th of June,
1870.   These being Majors C. B. Collins and
G. H. Harrison, and Captains R. B. Moody
and G. P. Strong.   And the offense they
were guilty of being merely that committed
by Lafayette, Steuben and De alb when
they espoused the cause of the American
Colonies in their struggle against Great
Britain.

In this movement, as usual, General RYAN
acted a vigorous and untiring part.   He was
then on duty in Washington.

In speaking of the energy and ability of
General RYAN in favor of Cuba, the late Vice .
President, Henry Wilson, said :

"I believe no truer patriot ever espoused
the cause of liberty.   In this struggle for recognition of Cuba's independence by this nation no man could have worked more zealous-
ly ; and it is a sad thing that he has failed in
his noble purpose."

THE CINCINNATI CONVENTION.

At the celebrated Republican Reform Con-
vention of 1872, by which Horace Greeley
was made a national target to be shot at by
both Democrats and Republicans, Gen. RYAN

was selected to represent the Cuban cause. He was warmly welcomed by the members of that honorable body, and permitted to proclaim to its members the wrongs heaped upon that suffering people by tyrant Spain. His speech was well received, and resolutions introduced favoring the recognition of Cuba's right to be free and independent. A synopsis of this address was telegraphed all over the country, and published in full in the Baltimore *Evening Journal*, Col. E. M. Yerger's able paper. The Colonel was a staunch friend of Cuba, but now he sleeps beneath the willows.

THE FANNIE EXPEDITION.

While the fight for recognition was going on in Washington, Generals Aguilera and Cespedes were organizing an expedition of arms and men to send to Cuba. When all was in readiness Gen. RYAN was telegraphed to hasten to New York to take charge of it, and to see it safely landed.

Monday, June 3, the telegram reached him, and by next morning he was at the magnificent Gilsey house up on Broadway, New York.

He met Generals Aguilera, Cespedes, Cisneros, Varona, and others, at breakfast, and conversed with them about the expedition.

On account of some difficulty as to the

ship's papers, the party did not get off until the 6th of June, 1872. The evening of that day General Cisneros and one of Gen. RYAN's aids called for him at Knickerbocker Club, and the three drove to Pier 20, where they met Gen. Aguilera and Senor Aldama. At 10 o'clock Gen. RYAN and the other expeditionists went aboard of the steamer Seth Low and sailed out of the bay.

General RYAN's Diary says that on that occasion the expedition "lost thirty-five good men through the rascality of Captain Brown the sailing master."

At 11 p. m., June 7, 1872, they met the C. L. Herrick, with arms and munitions on board. To her a transfer was made from the Seth Low, and the vessels parted company

The weather was raw and rough, according to General RYAN's notes, and by the third day nearly all the party were sick.

However, the General seems to have been in good spirits, his Journal being well sprinkled with careless and humorous remarks. The morning of June 8th he says:

"Last night slept on the soft side of a plank and covered with the *Sun*, *Herald* and *Tribune*. It rained during the night, and I woke up as wet as a 'biled' dish rag. Am fearfully sick, and most of our party ditto."

June 9th they came up with the John Drill and G. L. Howard having war supplies which were as rapidly as possible absorbed by the Herrick.

THE STEAMER FANNIE.

At midnight of the 9th they sighted the steamer Fannie, which was to land the expedition on the Island, and were soon alongside her.

The expedition was soon transferred to her and she then headed for her destination.

General RYAN dotted the following in his Journal June 16, 1872:

"Last night the weather was fearful. Old sailors thought we would be food for fishes. The waves rolled mountain high, and the wind was terrific. The Fannie is a regular old tub, and great indignation is felt at Capt. Brown for recommending such a miserable hulk. If a Spanish cruiser sights us we are gone up. Men sick, and grumbling about fresh water and spirits. Am hardly able to do duty."

"June 18.—Sudden change in weather. Beautiful sunset this eve; never saw anything so lovely. Old Sol went westward in a chariot of burnished gold, and left the clouds gilded with a halo of glory."

ATTEMPTED ASSASSINATION

On the morning of June 20, 1872, an attempt was made to murder General RYAN. He had been very sick during the night, and had fallen into a quiet sleep about 4 o'clock. He had scarcely become oblivious when he was awakened by feeling a sharp, cold sting in his left side. Being scarcely able to move he aroused his orderly, and investigated the matter. His clothes were found slit open for six inches across his side, near the left breast, and blood trickling from a wound corresponding in length. The Surgeon was immediately summoned. Upon examination the wound was found to be of no serious character. But if it had not been that the instrument of the assassin first struck the Masonic-military medal on his jacket that was thrown over him, there is scarcely a doubt that the steel would have done its work well. Notwithstanding that every measure was instituted for that purpose, no clue was ever discovered as to the would-be murderer, save that when the Fannie landed two of her crew deserted.

That the plot originated in New York, and was known to some one who wished General RYAN well, was evidenced by the fact that as he was going down the pier the evening he left a person dressed as an apple girl, no doubt a disguise, handed him a note, which he thrust into his pocket, intending to read it as soon as he got on board the vessel. After the attempt on his life he thought of the note and found it a warning, which read as follows :

"General, beware of the assassin. Remember there is a reward of $40,000 for your death. Be always on the alert.

"A FRIEND."

No doubt this was warning of an infamous Spanish plot to deprive the Cubans of their great American ally, the man who dared *retaliate* upon their enemies for the devish cruelties practiced upon them.

THE LANDING.

June 21, at 2 p. m., an attempt was made to land the expedition, but the threatening proximity of a Spanish war vessel made a change necessary, and the Fannie stood out from shore.

At 9 o'clock at night she went to open sea, it not being safe to land at Sagua.

After beating about until June 23, the expedition was finally landed at 3 in the morning, at Bird Rock.

In attempting to make a landing close to the shore, the vessel was run fast on the rocks.

On June 24th Gen. Peralta started to the interior with the expedition. Before leaving he and the Surgeon insisted on General RYAN returning to the States until he recovered his health. Being in such feeble health, and knowing it would be months ere he could do field duty, he concluded to take the Surgeon's advice.

That evening the Fannie was set on fire, and General RYAN, the Captain and crew took the small boats and started for Nassau. The weather became very stormy, and they were tossed about until June 27th, when they were picked up by the schooner Charles and taken to their destination.

June 29th they arrived in Nassau, where General RYAN was heartily welcomed by his many friends, among whom were Colonel Chance, and Mr. — Sargent and family.

On the 1st of July the steamer Crescent City arrived at Nassau, and General RYAN went on board of her. The Captain, whom the General called an impudent puppy, ordered him off, and became terribly excited, fearing that the fact of allowing the noted Cuban Chief on his decks would militate against him when he reached Havanna.

July 9th, while General RYAN was dining with those noble Cubans, Mrs. and General Quesada, a Spanish report reached him that the Fannie expedition had been captured, and all the men killed. This turned out to be a false rumor.

AT KEY WEST.

July 11th General RYAN left Nassau for

Key West on the schooner Express, and arrived there July 14th, at 12 m.   He received a warm reception from his Cuban friends and the officers of the American army and navy. During his stay he dined on board the United States war vessel Kansas, with Capt. Halfield, Lieut. White and Paymaster Beemish, three splendid gentlemen.

July 13th the General left for Cedar Keys on the steamer Tappatuck(?), Capt. C. W. Reed, and arrived there the evening of July 20th.   With him was a professed English capitalist, named Wm. Anderson, who subsequently victimized him and a number of people in Charleston and Savannah.

RETURN TO WASHINGTON.

From Cedar Keys General RYAN returned to Washington, via Atlanta, Ga.   At the latter city he tarried for a little rest, and his Journal mentions how kindly he was treated by the "noble-hearted Southerners of that war-battered place."

He arrived in Washington July 24th, and was met by his friend Capt. John W. Fenton at the depot with a carriage, who had him driven to his hotel, the Metropolitan, on Pennsylvania Avenue.   Shortly after his arrival his rooms were crowded with a host of admiring friends, who sympathized with him in his afflicted condition.

It was months before he entirely recovered from his sickness and the wound made by the dastardly assassin.

During Gen. RYAN's illness Capt. Brown, who commanded the Fannie, made a wanton attack upon him in the New York *Sun*, in which he accused him of cowardice in not remaining on the Island contrary to the advice of the Surgeon and Gen. Queralta.

General RYAN's reply to this slander was a scathing indictment of Capt. Brown as an enemy to Cuba, and a vile tool in the hands of the base Spaniards. The charges were so well supported by facts as to his treachery that he had to subside into ignominious silence, outside of endeavoring to shoulder the responsibility of his outrage against Gen. RYAN upon Senor Aldama, because at the time a little coolness existed between the latter and Gen. RYAN, on account of the General being a partisan of Gen. Quesada.

LETTER FROM COL. HARRY REEVES.

On the 20th of September, 1872, Colonel Harry Reeves wrote General RYAN a long and very interesting letter, which was published in the New York *Herald*. It was written at Cavalry headquarters, Vista Hermosa, and gave a complete review of the terrible struggle since the General left the Island. Its tone was very hopeful. The Colonel said that the army, and especially the Cavalry, was very anxious for the "devil's" return.

On account of General RYAN's reckless daring in battle he earned the sobriquet of *devil*, which clung to him throughout his career on the Island.

The letter also hoped that the report was true that the dashing General Kilpatrick was going to espouse the cause of Cuba.

This letter was written on all sorts of scraps of paper, with pencil, and ink made from berries. It is quite a curiosity, and is now in the possession of Col. J. Geo. Ryan, the General's brother.

ANOTHER JEALOUS SLANDER.

While to the public things seemed to be working harmoniously between the Cubans and their friends in New York the country was suddenly startled by a card in the public press denouncing General RYAN as a traitor to the cause of Cuba, and professing to act in her behalf without having the shadow of proper authority so to do. This slanderous document emanated from one S. M. Mayorga the interpreter of Senors F. V. Aguilera and Ramon Cespedes, Cuban Commissioners to the United States, and during their temporary absence from New York, and was without the semblance of authority.

It would be a difficult task to describe the

astonishment and anger of the General when he read the malicious slander. But as quick as possible he published a reply denouncing Mayorga as an infamous, lying, usurping, pretentious, jealous, mean scoundrel, who had presumed upon his hireling position to exert powers not delegated to his masters, and only vested in the Cuban Congress, by whose direct authority he, RYAN, was acting.

This scathing epistle fell heavily upon the head of Mayorga, who was immediately dismissed from his position on the return of the Commissioners.

General RYAN was so outraged at Mayorga's villainy that he threatened to go to New York and horse-whip him, which he would have done had he not apologized in the fullest manner.

Mayorga died in New York shortly after General RYAN was murdered. He was generally believed to have been a strong friend of Cuba, aside from his petty jealousy of some of his superiors.

It must be borne in mind that these personal difficulties never for a moment interfered with the glorious work in favor of poor Cuba's independence.

THE EDGAR STUART EXPEDITION.

The next expedition after that of the Fannie was the famous Edgar Stuart, which was organized by Generals Quesada and RYAN, and Colonel Aguera, the latter conducting it to Cuba, where it was safely landed about the middle of January, 1873. It was one of the finest organized. On his return from the dangerous adventure, the gallant Colonel received a grand ovation from his many friends 'n New York.

AN APPEAL TO THE NEGROES.

So that nothing might be left undone to attract the attention of the Congress of the United States towards Cuba, General RYAN made a strong appeal, in January, 1873, to the negroes of the District of Columbia in behalf of those who, when they unflurled their banner against Spanish tyranny, struck the chains from the limbs of half a million of God's creatures and declared them forever free. This was ably seconded by Hon. Fred. Douglas, and published in the *New National Era* of Washington, D. C., a journal edited by Mr. Douglas in the interest of the colored people of all nations. This had the effect of bringing about a large mass meeting, but through the free use of Spanish gold it was made to work inharmoniously. In consequence of this the whole matter fell lifeless to the ground, and Congress adjourned without giving the situation in Cuba more than a passing notice.

DEATH OF GEN. IGNACIO AGRAMONTE.

In March, 1873, Gen. RYAN lost a strong friend, and Cuba one of her truest patriots and bravest defenders, by the death of the noble, fearless and chivalric General Ignacio Agramonte, the l(r)c Commai de -in-Chief of Camaguey. He died while fighting at the head of his men, pierced by countless bullets. His body feel into the hands of the enemy, who mutilated it horribly, poured coal oil over it, and reduced it to a cinder by fire. In a letter published in the Pine Bluff, Arkansas, *Republican*, General RYAN spoke of his old comrade in the most glowing terms, elevating him to the highest pinnacle of bravery and fame. He was the first man to raise the flag of freedom in Camaguey, October 1868, simultaneously with the Cespedes uprising at Yara. His loss was a very serious blow to poor Cuba.

THE MYSTERIOUS SPANISH LADY.

One day in June, 1873, General RYAN received an anonymous letter, in a lady's chirography, requesting him to meet the writer at the postoffice at 5 p. m., and stating that he would recognize her by a parcel in her hand tied with broad blue ribbon. Seeing no particular harm in such a step, he determined to meet the author of the perfumed missive, and at the precise hour stepped into the office, and, as his Journal says, "met one of the most beautiful and queenly creatures that ever eyes beheld." They met as friends, and left the office chatting gaily. The lady led the way to the corner of Seventh and G streets, where they entered a carriage and drove to Georgetown, and stopped at a cozy little cottage, into which they went.

When they were seated in the handsomest of parlors, inhaling the sweet fragrance of lovely flowers, and refreshing themselves with delicious iced wine, the lady disclosed to General RYAN that she was the wife of a high Spanish official; that by means of a letter to her husband she had learned that the Spanish authorities had a number of very shrewd and unscrupulous spies on his (Gen. RYAN's) every action by night and day; that they were cognizant of his present plans for a large expedition to Cuba; and that they would most certainly capture it, and kill him and all on board. Then she told him that when she became aware of these facts she determined to warn him of his danger. She said one reason that impelled her to this course was that he had generously spared the life of her cousin whom he captured in the spring of 1870, near Puerto Principe. She then earnestly implored him to protect his life by not accompanying any more expeditions, that the Spanish government had determined upon his destruction, and that there

was little hope for him outside of Providenc
if captured. She further told him that she
would soon go to Havana, where her influence
was strong with the highest officials, and that
if he went on another expedition, and got
into any trouble she would make every sacrifice to get him out of it.

It might have been well for the gallant
RYAN if he had taken the advice of the bewitching lady. There is not a doubt but that
she was true in her professions of friendship
for him, because when she went to Havana
she wrote him a long and interesting letter
descriptive of her reception, which was one
of magnificence. She also mentioned how
he was looked upon by the officials in Havana, and the hate they bore him and all
Cuban rebels.

A few short weeks afterwards when poor
RYAN lay condemned to death, in Santiago's
gloomy prison, he thought of his beautiful
friend's warning and promise of aid. But it
availed nothing, for Butcher Burriel would
allow his victims no communication with
friends, and he was murdered without she
being able to raise her voice in his behalf.
When the public press announced the con-
pletion of Burriel's bloody work, the awful
news feel like a hideous pall upon her spirits
and threw deepest mourning around her heart
for many months afterwards.

She well remembers the last interview she had with *"Carrie."*

THE ILL-FATED VIRGINIUS EXPEDITION.

Now comes the sorrowful task of recording in a tangible form the events of the last blow our hero struck for Cuba's freedom, and which ended so tragically. Although the main facts in the bloody drama may have found a lodgment in the memory of the liberty-lovers of the world, still there are many interesting facts connected with that fiendish work that might never have reached the public if it were not that circumstances greatly favored the author of this humble book in his efforts to collocate reliable information, and to thereby add a chapter to the history of the times. The writer's ambition is to have the intelligent people of all nations fully aroused to the heinousness of the crimes that Spain has perpetrated against civilization in her barbarous and devilish treatment of the poor Cubans because of their attempt to throw off her galling and tyrannical yoke.

During the months of August and September the Cuban leaders of New York were cautiously perfecting their plans to send to their friends on the Island relief in men, munitions, arms, and army supplies of all kinds.

That Spanish spies might be thrown off their guard as to what was on the tapis, Gen.

RYAN went to Northern New York and made his headquarters at Schoharie, a delightful and very fashionable summer retreat, where he could communicate with his friends, and be safe in his interviews with those connected with the important project on hand.

While at Schoharie he, apparently, gave himself up to the full enjoyment of the many pleasures that lay in wait for him no matter where he roamed. And rumor even had it that he had given up the Cuban cause and surrendered to the lovely Miss Annie L. Gebhard, one of the most attractive of the many beautiful women of the charming little town, and a member of one of the oldest and most honorable families in the country. There appears to have been some foundation for this report, for after the dashing young cavalier's murder it was published that they were to have been married on his return from the ill-fated expedition. However, this was the gossip about him and Miss Belle Burche of Washington, and Miss Fannie A. Lockrow of New York, two lovely and accomplished ladies of the fashionable world. In reality he was entirely absorbed in the work that led him to the grave.

By the end of September all arrangements were perfected, and General RYAN returned to Washington. Generals Villegas, "Bembetta" Varona, Del Sol, Cespedes, Senor Aldama, one of Cuba's strongest friends, and others deeply interested in the cause, had done their work well, and the prospect looked bright for the safe landing of the most extensive expedition yet projected.

General Aguilera, one of the Cuban Commissioners, superintended the purchase of the extensive war materials, and had in his secret service, as aids, Colonels Jose Boitre, Salbadon Penedo, Oscar Varona, Augustine Santa Rosa, and young Euminio Quesada, son of Gen. Manuel Quesada.

And the heroic, war-worn naval veteran, Captain Joseph Fry, was to take command of the fleet steamer Virginius, then in Southern waters, and land the expedition; he having a short time before very successfully accomplished a like mission with her.

When everthing was in readiness for the departure from New York the hearts of all interested in the desperate venture beat high at the glorious prospect of bringing so much good cheer to their suffering brethren; and although fully aware of the dangers attending their mission, still they believed Fortune would not so favor their enemies as she subsequently did. But when treason and Spanish gold shake hands Fortune soon finds herself bound in iron fetters.

The evening of October 3rd, 1873, Gen. RYAN gazed for the last time upon the glories of Washington, the "city of magnificent distances," where he had drunk so deep of the cup of pleasure, and revelled so long in the delights of her enchanting society. He was suddenly summoned to New York, and like a true soldier responded immediately. He took a hurried leave of his friends, and by 10 at night was well on his way to the Empire city. Before departing he wrote a few lines to his brother, Colonel J. G., at Pine Bluff, Arkansas, telling him of his intended trip, and requesting him not to mention it publicly until he wrote by return steamer. He went off so hurriedly that he forgot to mail this letter until he reached New York. If he ever wrote by the return steamer it never reached his brother.

Because of some unlooked for delay the party did not get off from New York until October 6th. As General RYAN was hurrying to the vessel he was arrested for a debt of security, the party making oath he was going leave the State. It was a Spanish dodge to trammel his movements. However, it was decided to liquidate it, sooner than the expedition should be detained another day, while the court passed upon the matter.

That night the steamer Atlas swung loose from her moorings and sailed out to sea.

ARRIVAL AT KINGSTON, JAMAICA.

In due time the Atlas arrived at Kingston,

Jamaica, with her precious human freight, October 13th, after a very unpleasant voyage.

From that time until the party sailed for Cuba on the Virginius, General RYAN and his particular friends spent a most sumptuous and joyous time among the Jamaicans and the distinguished representatives of foreign countries. It was one long grand gala day; a happy bridal party, soon followed by the awful solemnities of a horrible butchery.

Before starting on the Virginius General RYAN wrote the following letter to General George W. Cook, Washington, D. C. It was dated Blundell Hall, Oct. 23, 1873:

"MY DEAR GEORGE—In one hour we leave for Cuba. This is quite sudden, as we did not expect to go until to-morrow, and I have just returned from the country. We arrived safely on the 13th inst. Had quite a storm on the 7th. All the provisions were washed overboard, and deck swept fore and aft. Captain Harris and the purser were badly injured, and we were a sea-sick set. The Captain pronounced it the severest hurricane he ever saw. For hours I thought we would all enjoy the novely of a bath in mid-ocean. Since our arrival we have had a splendid time—feast after feast and ball after ball. First a grand ball was given by the Peruvian Minister in honor of General Varona and myself. All the fashion and wealth

of the place were present. Mr. Governor
General Cordova and Judge Tichburn gave
others, and gay ones they were. The place
is filled with beautiful women and gay and
splendid fellows, generous to a fault and lib-
eral as princes. I must say that I never received such attention. I regret that want of
time will prevent me giving you a detailed
account of my adventures. I am as fat as a
bear and gay as a lark, and leave this place
with many regrets.

"Very truly, etc., W. A. C. RYAN."

LEAVING KINGSTON.

On the 23rd of October Capt. Fry signified that the Virginius was in readiness
to proceed on her mission, so all the party
embarked.

Quite a gay company of friends accompanied the adventurers for several miles to
sea, having in their wake a tugboat to take
them back.

A STARTLING ADVENTURE.

This farewell tribute of love came near
ending in a tragedy. As the party were
leaving the Virginius for the tugboat two of
them fell overboard into the boiling sea,
that was running high at the time. These
were Dr. Govin and another gentleman. As
soon as the dread alarm reached Gen. RYAN,

who had just stepped into his cabin, he hurried on deck, threw off his coat, jumped into the sea, and at the risk of his own life saved his two friends from a watery grave.

This heroic act was only one of a number in the short life of one of the bravest young hearts that ever pulsated in a freeman's breast.

On one occasion he saved the lives of four young ladies, capsized from a boat in front of Washington City, by similar coolness and unsurpassed courage. Among those also in danger, and whose life he saved, was a gentleman who had in several instances endeavored to, covertly, injure General RYAN in the estimation of some ladies. This fact was known to the General, but he did not allow it to influence him when his jealous enemy was in the act of drowning. This truly magnanimous and heroic part played by the General soon made a strong friend of his hitherto bitter foe.

Poor RYAN! he was ever ready to risk his life for those in distress.

AT PORT AU PRINCE—TAKING ON BOARD THE WAR MATERIALS.

On the 27th of October, 1873, the Virginius steamed into Port au Prince, Hayti, and there, beneath the secret shadows of night, took on board her war materials, consisting

of field artillery, rifles, pistols, sabres, machettes, and munitions of all kinds, and medicines, clothing, horses and accoutrements.

Notwithstanding the secresy of her movements, the Spanish consul became very much
alarmed when he discovered that the notorious Virginius was in port, and he created so
much disturbance because of her presence
that she was compelled to hurriedly go to
sea on the 28th of October.

THE FATAL TELEGRAM.

Immediately on the Virginius leaving Port
au Prince the Spanish Consul telegraphed to
Santiago de Cuba the fact of her suspicious'
movements. The famous Spanish war vessel'
Tornado was in port when the telegram was
received, and her commander, Senor Castillo,
at once weighed anchor, and commenced a
cruise, the result of which elevated him to a
very conspicuous place of honor in the history
of his country.

A strange coincidence may be here mentioned. The Virginius and Tornado were
built together in Scotland, by the same firm,
as Confederate blockade runners. They were
very fleet. After the war between the North
and South the Tornado was sold to the Peruvian government, and afterwards passed into
the hands of the government of Spain, and
was converted into a man of war. The Vir-

ginius passed into private hands, and her
name was changed from the Virgin to the
Virginius. She was used as a merchantman
until chartered by the Cubans as a blockade
runner, in July, 1873, when she successfully
landed Gen. Quesada's expedition from Aspinwall.

THE PURSUIT.

On the ever memorable evening of the 31st
of October, 1873, the Tornado sighted her
prey as she was heading for the "ever faithful isle."

About the same time the Virginius discovered the suspicious vessel, and believing it
must be a Spanish cruiser, immediately commenced retreating towards the coast of Jamaica. As soon as the Tornado discovered
the change of course she concluded that her
suspicions were correct, and that the fleeing
ship was none other than her old comrade,
the Virgin(ius). Then she immediately
crowded on all steam and sail, and began
the pursuit. The Virginius also fired up, and
strained every nerve to distance her relentless
enemy. Each vessel did its best, and soon
two long streams of fire and smoke stretched
along the horizon as the death struggle commenced.

Gradually the Tornado began to gain upon
her victim. This seemed unaccountable to
Captain Fry, as both vessel were of the exact

rate of speed before the Tornado had become so encumbered by her heavy armament, which would most certainly make her less rapid. This fact justifies the general belief that the engines of the Virginius had been tampered with by some traitor.

When those on board the Virginius discovered that she was losing ground the most intense excitement broke forth. Seeing this Captain Fry advised Generals RYAN and Varona to lighten the vessel by having the artillery, gun carriages, horses, heavy ammunition, and everything else calculated to retard her speed, thrown overboard, which was immediately done. But this did not seem to help matters much, while the excitement and confusion grew worse. Concluding that they would be captured, and knowing that themselves, and probably all on board, would be murdered, Generals Varona and RYAN advised the immediate

BLOWING UP OF THE VESSEL.

Captain Fry would not countenance this, stating that the ship's papers were all regular, and taken out for Port Limon, Costa Rica, and would be respected by the Spanish authorities; and that the only serious results of a capture would be a short detention and confinement, until the status of the vessel could be established.

This declaration had the effect of somewhat

allaying the fears of the crew, but did not change the opinions of Generals RYAN, Varona, Del Sol and Cespedes, as to their fate if captured.

By slow degrees the Tornado lessened the distance between herself and the Virginius, notwithstanding the latter exerted all her powers to keep out of cannon range.

By 10 o'clock the crisis came.

Boom, boom, boom, spoke the Tornado's guns in tones that fell like a pall upon those crowding the doomed ship's decks, while the heavy shot screeched over their heads and sent a chill to nearly all of their hearts.

The chase was at an end, and the summons to surrender was complied with immediately, Captain Fry believing that no Spanish tyrant would dare outrage the American government by injuring those sailing under her flag and properly credentialed. Alas! for such credulity. It soon appeared that Spain's minions dared commit one of the most heinous breaches of international law that ever disgraced humanity, and which challenged the horror of the civilized world.

THE CAPTURE.

In a few minutes after the Virginius hove to two Spanish officers, Don Angel Oetiz Monasterio and Don Enrique Pardo, with a detachment of marines from the Tornado, boarded her.

Captain Fry showed his papers to the boarding officer, and protested against the legality of his vessel's capture. The officer replied that he cared not what flag she carried, she was a pirate. Then turning to one of the marines he shouted :

"Take down that d—d rag, and hoist up our colors."

This was done, and the stars and stripes, the idol of all true Americans, was stretched on the deck and trampled beneath the feet of Spain's brutish hirelings.

Captain Fry remonstrated against the dastardly outrage, and told the insolent Spaniards that they would not dare to thus insult the American flag if the Virginius' crew and passengers were armed. The shameful conduct of the Spanish officers was testified to by Mr. King, one of the captured vessel's engineers, and a British subject, whose life was saved. This gentleman said that for some unaccountable reason the Virginius did not exceed eight knots an hour during the chase, when her usual speed was sixteen.

No further evidence is necessary to convince the most skeptical that the capture of the Virginius was due to base treachery.

For his remonstrance, Captain Fry and Mr. Rigo, General Del Sol's secretary, and eight others, were securely tied in the cabin.

Generals RYAN, Varona, Cespedes and Del

Sol having been immediately recognized by the boarding officers, were placed under a strong guard, and not permitted to speak.

The Spaniards were so intoxicated with joy at the capture that they hooted, howled, jeered and ranted in the most insane manner, and disgraceful in the extreme.

When the excitement had subsided General RYAN and the rest of the prisoners were transferred to the Tornado, and both vessels steamed for Santiago de Cuba, where they arrived on the 1st of November, 1873, at 5 o'clock p. m.

THE TRIAL—FOUND GUILTY OF PIRACY.

It would be an insult to justice to call the inquisition held on board of the Tornado a judicial affair that condemned to death Gen. RYAN, and the rest of the one hundred and fifty one persons captured on the Virginius, on the baseless charge of piracy. Nevertheless such it was styled, and Generals RYAN, Varona, Del Sol and Cespedes were selected as the first victims, their execution to take place at 6 o'clock on the morning of November 4th, 1873.

IN SANTIAGO'S PRISON—THE NIGHT BEFORE THE MURDER.

After the farce of a trial was over General RYAN, and Generals "Bembetta" Varona,

Jesus Del Sol, and Oscar Cespedes, were removed from the Tornado and placed in the
dismal jail of Santiago. As they passed
through the streets they were hooted and
jeered at by some of the large concourse that
had assembled to gaze on them. But they
heeded not their cowardly insults, and flashed
back scorn and defiance at the blood-thirsty
rabble of Butcher Burriel, the commander of
Santiago.

The prison into which the condemned men
were placed was solid, dismal, iron-bound,
dreary, silent and awe-inspiring. It was the
evening before their murder that they were
put into this gloomy abode, and the heavy
iron bars closed upon them.

The moralist will inquire how they spent
their last night on earth.

As heroes should. As soon as they were
informed of their fate they commenced writing letters of love, friendship and business.
This through, they gave themselves up to conversation with the Roman Catholic clergy,
who visited upon them the last rites of the
church. They loooked their fate squarely in
the face, and determined to meet it as only
those can who die for a great principle.

General Ryan wrote five letters, besides
his last will and testament. They were to
his brother in Arkansas, his mother in Chicago, Illinois ; Miss Belle Burche, Washing

ton, D. C.; Miss Annie L. Gebhard, Schoharie, New York, and General George W.
Cook, Washington, D. C. These were in
as firm a hand as if written when life seemed
most promising. The six were placed in one
package to be sent to General Cook, but by
some mistake it was directed to Gen. Geo.
W. *Smith*. Not being called for, it went to
the dead letter office, where the true owner
was discovered by Mr. England of that department. General Cook was then notified,
and he receipted for it. Afterwards he sent
the last precious missives to their several ad-
dresses. Eight months had now elapsed
since they were written.

The following are copies of the letters to
his brother and mother, and of the will:

PRISON, ST. JAGO DE CUBA, Nov. 3, 1873, 10:30 P.M.

MY DEAR BROTHER—At six o'clock to-morrow morning
my lamp of life will be exhausted, and the grave will
open to receive my cold and silent corpse The steamer
Virginius was captured off the coast of Jamaica on the
31st of October, three days ago, by the Spanish man-of-
Tornado. We were taken to this port—151 passengers and
crew—and Gen. B. Varona, M. Cespedes, bro her of President Cespedes Colonel Sol, and myself, were condemned
as Cuban soldiers, and condemned to death. As I wrote
you from Washington, General Geo. W. Cook has all my
trunks and papers, also a full power of attorney, which I
revoke in my will, and give all my property to you. See
Gen. Cook, settle my debts, and keep all the property. I
owe Governor Gibbs about $600; Gen. Cook $2,000. That
is about all. Anything that General Cook says will be all
right. He is my partner in the chrome and asbestos proper y, which I value at $100.000. He will act honorably
with you. Send the enclosed letter to our dear mother.

Do not neglect her, and God will bless and protect you. Farewell. dear brother.   W. A. C. RYAN.

N. B.—My ring, medal and charm-bullet, General Cook will send you. Destroy all my lady friends' letters.

COL. J. G. RYAN, Pine Bluff, Arkansas.

THE WILL.

Know all men by these presents that I, W. A. C. Ryan, being in sound mind, do make this my first and last will, giving all my property, real and personal, to my brother, John George Ryan. All my right, title and interest in and to all tracts or parcels of land in Montgomery county, State of Maryland, and containing chrome and asbestos, now appearing upon the rec rls in the names of William Loughridge and W. A. C. Ryan. All my interest in the copper mines on the Musselshell, in Montana ; my claim against the government, and my claim against W. A. Whittaker and James Thayer, and all property des· cribed in a power of attorney given to Geo. W. Cook, Oct. 3rd. 1873. My interest in Montana territory I value at $100,000, and the chrome and asbestos at $50,000. Gov. I. L. Gibbs is to receive six hundred dollars, and General Cook two thousand. My brother, John Geo. Ryan, shall do with the property as he may feel disposed. In testimony whereof I have caused my seal to be affixed this 3rd day of November, 1873.   W. A. C. RYAN.

Witness: Ismael Jose Bertbard.

THE LETTER TO HIS MOTHER.

MY DEAR MOTHER—Long ere this reaches you I will be in my cold and silent grave. The priests have just left us, and I am prepared to die. I do not fear death. I die as I lived, fearing nothing but the God above me. I left Kingston, Jamaica, on the steamar Virginius. She was captured by the Spanish man-of-war Tornado on the 31st of October, 20 miles from Jamaica. We were brought here, condemned as Cubans, and sentenced to be shot at six o'clock to-morrow morning—General B. Varona, M. Cespedes. Colonel Sol, and myself. The other passengers may get off. The steamer, when captured, had no arms on board. Dear mother, may God forgive me if I have ever offended you, or caused you one moment's pain. Say to my dear sister that I fondly love her, and deeply regret not being able to see her ere my departure from this earth.

Farewell, darling mother, for a short time ; we will soon meet my dear father in heaven. May God protect you, mother. Fondly your son, W. A. C. R.

As it has be doubted that Gen. RYAN received the last holy offices of the Roman Catholic church before his death, it is only necessary to refer to the unfortunate young hero's statement in his letter to his mother. He never forgot for a moment the church he was born in, even though he may not have lived up strictly to her doctrines. But he was no religious bigot. He never interfered with the opinions of others, and deprecated fanatical religious broils, and especially where they were calculated to keep Irishmen disunited.

When the good priests left the condemned, who did not feel like sleeping, Gen. Varona suggested that a song would drive away any ghastly gloom that had gathered around, and called upon General RYAN to give them "Hurrah for the next that dies," it being applicable to their wretched situation. This being agreeable to all, General RYAN sang in a clear, full, musical voice that grim, ghostly, demoniacal farewell of the British soldiers who were cut off from succor in some desolate region of the East Indies, and all perished by cholera. One of the number was an educated man, and he composed the shuddering refrain, which was sung with boisterous *sang froid* as each unfortunate stepped into eternity. The following are the last stanzas:

Who dreads to the dust returning?
  Who shrinks from the sable shore,
Where the high and haughty yearning
  Of the soul can sting no more?
No! stand to your glasses! steady!
  The world is a world of lies;
One cup to the dead already;
  Hurrah for the next that dies.

Cut off from the land that bore us,
  Betrayed by the land we find,
Where the brightest are gone before us,
  And the dullest are left behind.
Stand! stand to your glasses, etc.

As the last notes of the weird and startling song died upon the midnight air the quartette gave a long, loud, electrifying cheer for Cuba Libre, which echoed and re-echoed throughout the dismal prison, and was listened to by the awe-struck, astonished and bewildered sentinel. This man's heart was touched by the prisoners' dark situation. He noticed that they had no beverage to make the song a reality, and having a flask of good brandy he shared it with them, and they merrily drank the noble fellow's health, while tears of sympathy rolled down his bronzed cheeks.

THE EXECUTION.

Night passed away quickly, and the fatal morning found the condemned apparently as light-hearted as if preparing for a joyous fete.

The 4th of November, 1873, will never be forgotten while intelligence reigns king of

the world.   At five o'clock in the morning
the bells of the old historical town of Santiago began to toll mournfully.   It was the
signal of death, and the inhabitants commenced hurriedly assembling at the scene of
blood.

At twenty minutes to six the four martyrs,
Generals RYAN, Varona, Del Sol and Cespedes, were marched from the prison to the
place of execution, their hands being tied behind their backs.   A strong body of soldiers
formed the guard.   Along the route to

THE SLAUGHTER PEN

a number of ruffians hooted and howled, but
the great majority of those assembled preserved a respectful silence, apparently of
sympathy for the poor victims of Spanish
hate and tyranny.

The slaughter house to which they were
led is a low, square building, fronting south
of east, and the last one on the suburbs.   A
wall runs around this, which is flanked by a
wide ditch, upon whose brink hundreds of
Cubans have knelt to their death, and had
their blood and brains spattered on the
wall, while their quivering bodies rolled into ·
the filthy chasm.

Before this blood-stained and bullet-batter-
ed wall General RYAN and his three comrades
were halted.   They were cool, calm and col-

lected, with a smile of defiance and scorn
overspreading their bronzed faces. General
RYAN seemed as indifferent as if nothing extraordinary was about to transpire. The
awful shadow of death hanging over him left
not the faintest shadow upon his features,
but instead a bright glow reigned in kingly
majesty over all.

As the prisoners halted upon the brink of
the ditch into which their lifeless bodies were
soon to roll, to be trampled by the iron hoofs
of Spanish dragoons, the guard formed three
sides of a square around them, the wall mak-
the fourth. Then the death warrant was
read, and the condemned were asked if they
had anything to say.

General RYAN answered for himself and
comrades briefly, as follows :

"Before high heaven I solemnly protest
against this high-handed act as a murder
most foul, and a gross insult to the American
nation, from under the protection of whose
flag we were defiantly dragged to this unau-
thorized and unjustifiable butchery. But as
Spain measures to us, so shall it be measured
to her. Our base murder, this dark deed
against civilization, will strengthen the cause
for which we willingly die, and will brace the
nerves of our brothers to strike stronger
blows for their liberty, and revenge for our
deaths. Farewell, friends. Success to dear
Cuba. She will yet be free. We are ready."

As these words fell from the young hero's lips the silence was intense, and the prophetic speech could be heard throughout the vast crowd, and it remained unbroken until the officer ordered the victims

TO KNEEL AND BE BLINDFOLDED.

Generals RYAN and Varona protested against this, and then an attempt was made to force them on their knees. But as they still struggled, and pleaded to be allowed to die standing, the officer very humanely granted their request.

The fatal moment had now arrived. The death kneel rang out solemnly from the old, weather-beaten tower. It was the dread hour of six, when four brave spirits were to be suddenly hurled into eternity.

At the summons Generals Cespedes and Del Sol calmly knelt down, facing the blood-stained wall.

But Generals RYAN and Varona stood up firm and erect, not a muscle quivering, and no sign of fear visible upon their noble countenances, as they gazed upon the mute crowd, who seemed horrified at the awful tragedy about to be enacted.

The priests and a few friends then took an affectionate farewell of the condemned, and the last act of the bloody play was commenced.

The firing party now took position, the signal was given, a loud and prolonged report followed, and a shower of lead hurled the four souls suddenly before their God. Gen. RYAN was not instantly killed, so the commander of the guard stepped forward and thrust his sword through his heart, and ended his misery. This was an act much condemned by the general public, but when it is looked at in a humane light the official deserved commendation instead of blame for putting an end to the gallant fellow's great sufferings. The others died easy.

When life had fled from poor RYAN a friend stepped forward and cut off a few of his beautiful brown curls, and removed from his mangled breast a badge of the order of the Grand Army of the Republic, which were, together with his seal ring, medal, and the bullet cut out of his hip at Newbern, North Carolina, and worn as a charm, sent to the care of his trusted friend General Geo. W. Cook, Washington, D. C., for his brother, Colonel J. G.

HORRIBLE FINALE.

This had scarcely been accomplished before the pent up passions of the fiendish portion of assemblage broke forth in devilish fury. They rushed through the ranks of the soldiers, who were leaving the bloody scene, and pounced upon the lifeless bodies like beasts of prey, howling, screaming and cursing all the time in the most revolting manner.

They cut off their heads, placed them on poles, and marched with them into the city, yelling and hooting as they went.

Then the heavy dragoons came down upon the bleeding, headless trunks, and ground them into the mire beneath the iron hoofs of their maddened steeds. The artillery followed, and the ponderous wheels crushed into an unrecognizable mass what had been left unbruised by the brutish horsemen.

This over, the crushed and bleeding corpses were thrown into a cart, and from it pitched into a hole, and the ground levelled over them.

The horrible and disgusting drama was now at an end, and one of the blackest crimes ever committed by a nation pretending to be civilized was placed upon record against Spain, and one of her devilish minions, *Butcher Burriel*, became immortalized as the prince of cold-blooded murderers.

Spain's cup of pleasure was now full. Gen. RYAN, one of poor Cuba's best friends, was no more, and wild rejoicing was had wherever her blood-stained banner waved.

The hellish deed was done. The American flag had been trampled and spit upon, and humanity outraged.

But what cared fossilized, tyrant Spain for the United States, or the rest of the world! Nothing. She had accomplished her bloody work, so far, well, and laughed defiance at those who might dare dispute her right to murder and outrage at pleasure.

Still the blood-thirsty old fiend was not yet satisfied. She must have more blood.

MURDER OF CAPT. FRY AND THIRTY-SIX OTHERS.

When the four great leaders had been silenced forever, and laid beneath the earth in their gore, the murderers breathed freely, and revelled in delight for three days. Then their hearts ached for more blood, a wholesale butchery, and the gallant, heroic, noble and chivalrous Capt. Joseph Fry, the commander of the ill-fated Virginius, and thirty-six of her passengers and crew, were led out and slaughtered in the same manner as Gen RYAN and his three heroic companions. The deportment of Capt. Fry and his unfortunate comrades was grand to behold. They died like true martyrs, and blessed Cuba with their last breath. This horrible deed occurred on the 7th of November. Many were not killed by the first fire, and these were bayoneted to death in a brutal and shocking manner, making the spectacle truly frightful.

The names of the murdered were Capt. Joseph Fry; William Barnard, first mate; James Flood, second mate; and seamen C.

Harris, John Bosa, B. P. Chamberlain, Wm. Kose, Ignacio Duenas, Antonio Deloyo, Jose Manuel Teiran, Ramon Larramendi, Eusebio Gariza, Edward Day, J. S. Trujillo, Jack Williamson, Porfirio Corvison, P. Alfaro, Thomas Craig, Frank Good, Paul hunrer, Barney Herrald, Samuel Card, John Brown, Alfred Haisell, W. J. Price, Geo. Thomas, Ezekiel Durhan, T. Walter Williams, Simon Broyeur, Leopold Larose, A. Arci, John Stewart, Henry Bond, Geo. Thompson, Jas. Samuel, Henry Frank, and James Read.

On the 8th of November this bloody list was lengthened by the murder of eleven more poor fellows, making in all *fifty-two* who had fallen because of their devotion to the cause of suffering Cuba. Distinguished among these martyrs were Col. Jose Boitrl, Eminio Quesada, son of General Quesada, and only seventeen years of age; Captain Salbadon Penedo, Colonel Oscar Varona, and Augustine Santa Rosa, all of whom accompanied General RYAN from New York on the steamer Atlas to join the Virginius at Kingston, Jamaica. Oscar Varona was the brother of General "Bembetta" Varona, General RYAN's great friend.

ARRIVAL OF THE NIOBE.

This last horrible chapter had scarcely been enacted, and preparations completed for the murder of the remaining ninety-nine prisoners, already condemned, when the Brit'sh man-of-war Niobe steamed into port, and her gallant commander, Sir Lambton Lorraine, on learning the awful news, demanded that the bloody work should immediately stop, proclaiming that he would jealously protect the interests of the United States until one of her vessels arrived, and threatened to bombard the town if any attempt was made to continue the frighful programme of blood, or to in any way harm one of the prisoners.

Butcher Burriel quailed before this peremptory demand, and had to bend his knee to the bold Briton, whose dauntless courage saved from a shocking death the rest of the doomed men, and thereby immortalized himself in the hearts of every freeman throughout the world. All honor to the noble fellow. Poor Cuba, and the patriotic world, bows in homage at his shrine, and his name is written in characters of gold upon every liberty-loving breast throughout the broad universe. And his fame will never die, notwithstanding the fact that the Congress of the United States refused to pass a vote of thanks to him for his chivalrous conduct in protecting the honor of the nation, and in saving from slaughter ninety-nine helpless human beings. But this dissenting act of the majority of Congress did not reflect the sentiments of the great body of the American people, no more than did the puerile acts of her officials at Washington represent the wishes of the nation at the terrible outrage upon her flag having been allowed to go unpunished. *O tempora, O mores!* Shades of Andrew Jackson! and the sons of 1776! How the spirits of the noble departed must have wept as they gazed upon the truculent part played by those entrusted with the keeping of the honor of the country christened in war and baptized with patriotic blood, to a barbarous nation that heaped upon her the most monstrous insults.

It was not the murder of General RYAN, who had fought four years, and spilt his blood for the Union, that, alone, aroused the indignation of the American people. It was the infamous insult offered to the flag their fathers fought to maintain. This is why the people North, South, East and West, cried in thunder tones for revenge for Spain's heinous crime. And it is because they were not allowed an opportunity to wipe out this outrageous insult that the noble and patriotic sons of this glorious Union now hold down their heads in sadness, and weep that the heads of the government had basely deserted their post of trust when tyrant Spain spat in their faces, trampled upon their honor, and laughed at their pallid looks.

THE MURDERERS' PURPOSE.

To show that Butcher Burriel intended,

from the moment of their capture, to murder as speedily as possible all those found on the Virginius, it is only necessary to mention the startling fact that the fiend *would not allow* tidings of his bloody work to pass over the telegraph wires to the outer-world until after the gallant Sir Lambton Lorraine made him halt in his devilish career.

Up to this time the American and British Consuls were held in their residences as prisoners, by Devil Burriel's myrmidons, and not allowed to discharge the functions of their offices. Notoriously, it would seem, was this the case as to the representative of the United States, who was treated most shamefully, his life being threatened several times.

It was not until the 8th of November— eight days after the capture of the Virginius, and four subsequent to the murder of Gen. RYAN and his three comrades, that news of the frightful outrage reached the United States, and that only through the energy of American journalists in Havana.

No *official* news of the capture, and the first four murders, reached Washington until the 10th of November. At least such was the substance of an answer to a telegram of inquiry that Col. J. G. Ryan sent to Secretary Fish. This fact goes to prove one of two things: first, that the Spanish authorities grossly trammeled the American Consul; or, second, that the latter was criminally negligent in his duties.

The first appears to have been the true status of affairs. And this is why the people of the United States felt that their country was doubly outraged, and made them clamor wildly for revenge.

When it became an indisputable fact that the Virginius had been captured and General RYAN butchered, the appalling news fell upon his relatives and friends with crushing effect. They were shocked, stunned, paralyzed by the awful tale of blood, and thrown into a gloom so dark and ghastly that no sun of happiness can ever dispel the black traces of woe. The blow was terrible to his fond mother and sister, whom he dearly loved. They were stricken down, and it was many months ere there was any hope of their recovery. And the calamity threw a deep veil of gloom and heart-rending sorrow over the murdered hero's two brothers. For three long weeks after he received official news of the bloody tragedy, Colonel J. G. was prostrated with brain fever, and it took all the skill of his eminent physicians, Drs. Holcombe & Wright, and the tender care of his friend Col. Chas. G. Newman, and family, to restore him to health. It is said that the shocking murder of his brother cast a shadow over his heart that will abridge his life many years, and make it less sunny and joyous.

And there were other hearts and heads that ached when the intelligence of the fiendish massacre reached them—heads and hearts of both lady and gentlemen friends throughout the American continent who admired the noble young hero, and in whose loving hearts his fame will ever hold a hallowed place.

But he had been ruthlessly torn from relatives and friends, cruelly murdered by Spanish tyrants, was lost to them forever, and nothing was left them to do but to mourn that the gay, dashing, brave and handsome Gen. "Whack" RYAN would never again gladden their eyes on earth.

THE AMERICAN PRESS AND STATESMEN ON THE MASSACRE.

When the news of the brutal massacre of a number of the passengers and crew of the Virginius became a fact the press of the country, with a few unimportant exceptions, raised its mighty voice for prompt and speedy revenge for the horrible butchery and the outrage heaped upon the American flag, and called upon the government to at once recognize Cuba's independence. They stigmatized Spain's crime as the most heinous that ever blackened the record of a nation.

And such learned and able statesmen as the late Hon. Reverdy Johnston, and the late Vice President Wilson, arraigned Spain in the same just way for her damnable work of blood. Notwithstanding all this, and the storm of the people's rage that rolled itself like an avalanche against the White House and Congress, the foul murderess was permitted to go free by mockingly saluting the flag she grossly insulted, and promising to pay $2,500 to the families of each of the victims of her tyrannical wrath.

And the Virginius was accidentally(?) sunk, that litigation might be stopped in that direction. Thus ending one of the most disgraceful farces that ever stained the fair reputation of a nation established by the purest patriots that ever struck a blow for liberty, leaving her to be scoffed at by the bloodthirsty country that caused her degradation, and which promoted to high position Butcher Burriel for playing his villainous part so well.

But what mattered it all. The life of the gallant RYAN and his brave companions, and the honor of the American nation, amounted to nothing so the pockets of government pets were filled with Spanish gold.

The public press, while dealing with the main points of the Virginius horror, never for a moment forgot to honor the noble, chivalrous and gentlemanly character of General RYAN. Some administration organs were exceptions to the rule, they stigmatizing him

as a *filibuster*, in their ignorance forgetting
that, in attempting to cast a slur upon him,
they were blackening the records of Amer-
ica's idols—Lafayette, Steuben, De Kalb,
Pulaski and Kosciusko—who had acted in
the same manner as General RYAN did when
they entered the service of the United States,
in their fight to throw off the yoke of Great
Britain, before any country had recognized
their independence.   "Wherein, then,"
asked 'Soloman Sias,' in the Schoharie, N.
Y., *Republican*, "is the difference between
Lafayette and RYAN? Simply in the fact
that Lafayette lived until the country he came
to assist won her acknowledged independence," while General RYAN was murdered
as poor Cuba was rocking in the throes of
her fierce struggle for the same great boon.

And the same writer continues: "When
we fail to condemn the horrible murder of
General RYAN, or cease to admire his efforts
for Cuba's liberty, let us strike from the
pages of history the name of Lafayette and
the other noble *foreigners* who fought for
the freedom of the United States when they
were *unrecognized* by any of the nations of
the earth."

CONCLUSION.

The long narrative of Gen. RYAN's eventful life and tragic death has now been told,
and though never so imperfectly, still the

author feels satisfied with his humble efforts to do justice to the memory of his martyred hero, as well as to make his book acceptable to the general reader. So, after giving abridged sketches of the lives of Generals Varona, Cespedes, Del Sol, and Captain Fry, and alluding to what became of the personal effects General RYAN left in Washington, and touching on other interesting matters relating to him, he will say *au revoir* to his indulgent readers.

THE LATE GEN. GEO. A. CUSTER ON GEN. RYAN.

General Geo. A. Custer, the brave, fearess soldlier, and elegant gentleman, who, with his Spartan command, was massacred in June 1876, on the Big Horn, Montana Territory, by Sitting Bull and his savage Sioux, was a great admirer of General RYAN. When he heard of his foul murder he said:

"Poor RYAN, he was a gallant fellow, a splendid officer, and a gentleman without a blemish. Cuba lost her best friend when he fell. His dashing figure, chivalric bearing, handsome face, and elegant manners, made him a favorite wherever he went."

Other illustrious men replied to the author's interrogatories in the same eulogistic strain; and the same sweet refrain came to him from every region of the country—from the icy-fields of his hero's birth-place, and the lovely orange groves of the Gulf-washed

Sunny South—where the young martyr's fame had reached.

GEN. RYAN'S PERSONAL EFFECTS.

General RYAN had elegant rooms over Chas. P. Gautier's fashionable restaurant on Pennsylvania Avenue, Washington, D. C. After his murder, his friend, General George W. Cook, Colonel Aiken of the *National Republican*, and others, visited the apartments, and Gen. Cook took possession of all they contained that belonged to Gen. RYAN. This occurred on the 15th of November, 1873. Among the effects were a magnificent and very valuable sword, a present to the General; a blue silk banner, presented to him by the Cuban ladies of New York; and a Scrap Book containing most every newspaper reference to the General during his public career. On these articles Colonel John Geo. Ryan placed great value. When he arrived in Washington, and General Cook turned over to him his brother's effects, these were *missing*, and the General could not account for either of them, save that Colonel Aiken had borrowed the Scrap Book. The Colonel protested that he had returned it to the General. All this seemed very strange to Colonel Ryan, and if General Cook had not been such a strong friend of his brother he would have concluded that something was criminally wrong.. When Colonel Ryan left Washington he placed the matter in detective Coomes' hands to hunt up the missing things. The banner is still unaccounted for, but the Scrap Book has been traced to one of Colonel Aiken's friends, and General Cook found the sword in a pawn-broker's shop. This was the latest news recived from Capt. John W. Fenton, of Washington, by Colonel Ryan, in July 1876.

Another thing seems strange. The medal ring, charm-bullet and compass, sent from Santiago, to the care of General Cook, have not yet reached Colonel Ryan.

VARONA, CESPEDES, DEL SOL, AND FRY.

GEN. "BEMBETTA" VARONA was a native of Cuba, and born in Puerto Principe in 1845, and was 28 years of age when he was murdered. He was highly educated, and a gentleman without a peer. His family was one of the best on the Island. He was one of the first to join the Insurgents, and did valuable service up to the time of his death. He was captured once, but miraculously made his escape. He was a General of Division. He was tall, well made, with black eyes and hair, handsome, chivalrous, courteous, and recklessly brave. He and General RYAN were stanch friends.

GEN. JESUS DEL SOL was thirty-four years old at the time of his death. He was a Cuban statesman, and gallant soldier. He hated Spain, and used all his energies to see Cuba freed from her tyrannical grasp. His wife died soon after the commencement of the Revolution. He left four orphan children in the United States to mourn his loss. No braver man ever died for liberty.

PEDRO CESPEDES, a younger brother of the late Cuban President, who was captured and murdered by the Spaniards in 1874, was born in Bayamo, in the Eastern portion of Cuba. At the time of his execution he was fifty years old. For his country he gave up, like his compatriots, wealth, ease and luxury, and at last his life. He occupied both civil and military positions of importance and honor. He was a gallant soldier and a perfect gentleman.

CAPTAIN JOSEPH FRY, the commander of the ill-fated Virginius, was only forty years of age when he was ruthlessly sent into eternity by the fiendish Spaniards. He was a native of Florida, and was born in Tampa Bay. His family was very aristocratic. At an early age he determined upon the navy as a profession. Accordingly he presented himself before President Tyler, and asked to be, and was, sent the U. S. Naval Academy at Annapolis, from which he grduated with honors. He served as a Captain in the United States navy until the breaking out of the great Rebellion, when he resigned, and joined the Confederacy, and served in her army and navy during the war with distinction and honor. He was as brave a man as ever drew a sword for principle. He entered the Cuban blockade service from pure necessity. The reverses of the war made him poor, as it did all true Confederates, and he was forced to accept any legitimate business calculated to furnish a support for his much beloved wife and children. He died the hero, soldier, and christian; and left behind a record that those looking for honor and fame will ever try to emulate.

SECRET SOCIETIES.

It is a question whether or not Gen. Ryan was a Mason. But there is one fact that sustains the belief that he was; and that is this: among his papers was found a notification to appear before a New York lodge for initiation into the mysteries of that sublime order.

He belonged to the Grand Army of the Republic, and was a member of Winthrop Post, New York.

He was also Grand Khedive of the Ancient Order of Egyptian Monks.

> "Now lies he low—no more to hear,
> The victor's shout or clashing steel
> No more of war's rude cares to bear,
> No more kind sympathy to feel.
> No more he charges with the host,
> The thickest of the battle-field;
> No more to join in victory's boast,
> No more to see the vanquished yield."

FINIS.

www.ingramcontent.com/pod-product-compliance
Lightning Source LLC
Chambersburg PA
CBHW031400020726
47499CB00005B/1465